The Dark Beneath

ALAN GIBBONS

A Dolphin
Paperback

First published in Great Britain in 2003
as a Dolphin Paperback
by Orion Children's Books
a division of the Orion Publishing Group Ltd
Orion House
5 Upper Saint Martin's Lane
London WC2H 9EA

Reprinted 2004

A catalogue record for this book is
available from the British Library

Typeset at The Spartan Press Ltd,
Lymington, Hants

Printed in Great Britain by
Clays Ltd, St Ives plc

ISBN 1 84255 097 7

To the children and teachers of Knowsley, Merseyside

Part One
WATCHERS

One

Today I shot the girl I love.

They had a name for it round Marsham village. They called it the refugee summer.

Imogen Bayliss broke off clearing the breakfast dishes in the dining room of the Old Marsham Inn and snorted. She glared at the men on table five. Listen to them going on! About foreigners swamping the country, about the country being a soft touch! Oo-ooh, never heard that one before! Honestly, could they be more unoriginal? PC they weren't. What did they know about anything anyway? The oiks weren't even local. To Imogen, they were just a trio of tabloid-reading stereotypes: the cocky Cockney, the chirpy Scouser and the . . . what was the third one meant to be? The non-descript Midlander – yes, that'll do.

Imogen tossed back her blonde hair. She wasn't aware of the pair of ice-blue eyes that watched her. If she had been they might have distracted her from her thoughts. Because they were the eyes of a predator.

But Imogen, blissfully unaware of being watched, carried on regardless. She huffed. She shook her head. It had always been hard for her to keep her thoughts to herself. She had been brought up to speak her mind and believe in the importance of her opinions. Her parents were university people. Children of the Sixties, or maybe the early Seventies, they had a long list of causes under their belt. Anti-apartheid, anti-globalisation, CND – they'd supported them all. Imogen had grown up skipping happily in her parents' footsteps, protesting about the new Marsham bypass (tree-huggers, the local rag called them) or running a jumble sale for Kiddington Women's Refuge. Little Imogen's blonde curls had featured in more than one edition of the *Marsham Observer* as she grew up.

To her parents, Imogen was a bright, precocious, independent girl. Some of her teachers thought differently. Too full of herself, they would say from time to time. A bit of a madam. But here, on this summer's day, all Imogen knew was that these men were stupid. Refugee summer indeed!

While she was clearing the last of the dishes, she found herself clattering the cutlery with uncharacteristic vigour. She knew by their conversation what they meant, those three men who had just finished their full English breakfasts. It was pretty obvious they would have preferred a *no refugee* summer.

Imogen forced herself to keep her lips zipped. She was forced to make her protest the only way she could, setting up such a racket with the cutlery and crockery that their voices trailed off. Suddenly those ice-blue predator's eyes weren't the only ones looking at her.

'Somebody got out on the wrong side of the bed this morning,' said the man nearest her.

Imogen frowned and did her best to ignore him.

'We haven't done something to upset you now, have we, gorgeous?'

The speaker, a stocky, suntanned man in T-shirt, shorts and steel toe-capped boots, peered at Imogen's creased brow. She smelt sweat and stale smoke.

4

'Is it something we said?'

Imogen shook her head. She was aware of her new boss, Barry Hewlett, watching her closely. Her flesh crimped.

'No,' she murmured.

Getting fired from her job on the very first day would be a bad idea. Mum would be bound to start in on her: *You expect everything to drop in your lap.* Well, Imogen wasn't going to sit through *that* lecture. Grin and bear it, she told herself.

'Well, thank goodness for that. We can't have a pretty young thing like you getting herself in a tizzy, can we, boys? What's your name anyway?'

Imogen told them. She swept the three men with a brief glance. Their fluorescent green jackets with the legend 'Kiddington B' hung over the backs of their chairs. Kiddington B was the power station further down the coast. Another of the Bayliss family's former campaigns, nuclear power. *It'll cost you the Earth.* It hadn't yet, but it was a good line anyway.

They were smiling broadly, clearly enjoying Imogen's discomfort, except one of them who was making a show of reading his newspaper.

'Let me introduce you to my colleagues,' the stocky man said.

Out of the corner of her eye Imogen saw Barry Hewlett's expression relax.

'I'm Mickey Wise.' His accent was estuary English. 'This is Peter Riley.'

'All right there, sweet cakes?' said the shaven-headed thirty-year-old in a strong Liverpool accent.

Imogen listened to the exaggerated twang and wondered about professional Scousers, but she kept her thoughts to herself.

'And last but not least,' said Wise, cocking an amused eyebrow, 'may I introduce The Professor.'

He was still buried in his newspaper. Imogen could now see it was the *Times*. He roused her curiosity.

'Meet Gordon Craig. He's the mastermind of our little operation.'

Craig scowled. He didn't like having his leg pulled.

'Gordon doesn't belong with us horny-handed sons of toil,' said Wise. 'He's what they call . . .' – cue posh accent – 'an intellectual.'

Craig's frown deepened.

Imogen felt sorry for him. He wore glasses and his hair was thinning in that patchy, unkempt way that seemed to make fun of its owner. There was a whiff of disappointed hopes about him. He must be the continual butt of their jokes – two's company, three's a crowd, she thought. But at least he deflected their attention from her.

She really needed this job, as much for the independence it would afford her as for the money. Her parents were lovely and all, but sometimes they stuck to her like cling-film.

'So what brings a girl like you to a place like this?' Riley asked.

'Summer job,' Imogen answered. 'I've just finished my GCSEs.'

'I see,' said Wise, once again assuming the posh accent. 'So what does that make you, fifteen?'

'Sixteen.'

'Sweet sixteen, eh? What about that, boys? Hanother hintellectual in the making. How many subjects did you do?'

'Ten.'

'Ten GCSEs!'

Imogen managed a half-smile. To her astonishment, Wise seemed genuinely impressed.

'So how do you think you did?' he asked, his mocking temporarily suspended.

'I don't know. OK, I think.'

'OK?' said Wise. 'I bet you sailed through them. Clever *and* beautiful.'

This time Imogen could only manage a quarter-smile. He'd resumed his teasing and she didn't like it, just as she didn't like the smell of perspiration and smoke.

'Leave the girl alone,' said Craig. 'It's time we went anyway.'

'Your word is our command, Professor,' said Wise, snapping to attention.

He squeezed Imogen's shoulder as he went past. She felt the weight of his hand, his thick calloused fingers. Sweat from his palm blotted her sleeve. Something about him made her very uncomfortable.

'You have to watch the Professor,' Wise said with a wink. 'Hidden depths, my darling. Hidden depths.'

Imogen was more worried about Wise's visible shallows.

'I'll remember that,' she said.

They headed for the door and Imogen breathed a sigh of relief.

'Creeps!' she muttered.

The ice-blue eyes fixed her the way a headlight catches a rabbit in its beam.

Finally aware that somebody was watching her, Imogen felt a heat rash spread over the back of her neck. She turned, glimpsing a figure. Oh no, not Mr Hewlett! If he had overheard . . .

But it wasn't Barry Hewlett. It was somebody she hadn't seen before. She only glimpsed him for a moment but he reminded her of . . .

Oh, this was crazy!

. . . a ghost.

I watched her from the window. That's when I shot her.

*

7

Imogen stared at the empty doorway.

Was I dreaming? she wondered.

Those men had good and spooked her, especially the one called Mickey Wise. She'd never met anybody quite like him before: boorish, opinionated and . . . rancid. But it wasn't just a matter of being thrown by Wise. She was sure – well, pretty sure – that somebody else had been watching her from a distance. Sure too that the stranger had a ghostlike quality.

Shoving the puzzling thought to the back of her mind, Imogen stacked the breakfast things on her tray and made her way to the kitchen. She met Barry Hewlett coming the other way. She noticed that his shirt had come out of his trousers – something to do with his middle-aged spread. His developing paunch bulged over a tightly-fastened belt.

'Did you have a nice little chat with The Boys?' he asked.

'The Boys?' Imogen repeated. 'Oh, you mean the ones on table five.'

'Got to keep them sweet, Imogen,' said Hewlett. 'The Boys are our best guests. They're on a long-term contract at Kiddington B. They'll be staying with us five days a week for the next six months. Without their custom . . .' His face slackened. '. . . I dread to think what would happen to the business.'

Wonderful, thought Imogen. Don't tell me I've got to be nice to that bunch of losers every day until I go back to school. For the sake of *the business*. Never had Sixth Form seemed more inviting.

'They seem to have taken quite a shine to you,' Hewlett said. 'That's good. You'll probably earn yourself a few tips.'

Imogen forced a smile.

'Anyway,' said Hewlett, tucking his shirt-tail back in his pants and tugging self-consciously at the waistband, 'I've got to get on. It's time for Trixie's walk.'

'Trixie?'

Hewlett indicated a white poodle waiting patiently in the corner. Rheumy eyes looked briefly at Imogen, then – adoringly – at Hewlett.

'You know where the dishwasher is, don't you?'

Imogen nodded and Hewlett turned to go, Trixie clattering eagerly after him.

'Oh, Mr Hewlett.'

He gave an impatient sigh.

'Yes?'

'I thought I saw somebody.' She laughed self-consciously. 'I know this sounds stupid, but I thought it was a ghost.'

It was Hewlett's turn to laugh.

'Oh, there's a ghost at Old Marsham all right,' he said. 'That'll be my step-son. Anthony, where are you?'

There was a noise from the hallway.

'Come on out, Anthony. She won't bite.'

Hewlett turned to Imogen.

'He's a bit shy.'

Raising his voice again, he called down the corridor.

'Stop skulking out there and come and meet the new member of staff.'

Imogen turned to see the newcomer. He looked about fourteen, a couple of years younger than she was. He was quite tall and slim, but that wasn't what drew her attention. Anthony had snow-white hair and a complexion that was more drained of colour than simply pale. He wore glasses and behind the lenses his blue eyes flickered from side to side.

'Albinism,' said Hewlett, by way of explanation. 'It means—'

'Yes,' Imogen said, 'I've heard of Albinism. Lack of pigment in the skin, isn't it?'

'What about my eyes?' Anthony said, speaking for the first time. 'I bet you don't know the name for that.'

9

The words came out as a challenge. Imogen shook her head.

'The quiver,' Anthony told her, 'is called nystagmus.'

He seemed glad to get the explanations out of the way, as if he had been wondering how to break the ice.

'Nice to meet you,' said Imogen.

She reached out her hand. He stared at it for a moment or two before taking it.

Whatever the opposite is of a hearty squeeze, this was it. It was like shaking hands with . . . a ghost. His touch glided over her palm then drifted away again.

Anthony gave a brief nod of the head.

'Yes,' he said. 'You too.'

'Well, well,' said Hewlett, entertained by the encounter. 'I do think he's taken with you, Imogen. First The Boys, now Anthony. All those conquests in one day. I'll have to keep my eye on you, Imogen. I think you're a bit of a heart-breaker on the quiet.'

Imogen glanced away. Creep! She didn't like Hewlett. She didn't like his flabbiness and she didn't like his lame sense of humour. At the mention of the word heart-breaker she couldn't stop the colour flying to her cheeks. Anthony too averted his eyes. This time there was no colour.

I didn't kill her. You don't kill the one you love. That would be cruel. Self-defeating too. No, I just shot her – a way of making her mine.

Imogen was putting the last of the dishes away in the cupboard when Victoria Hewlett appeared. She had interviewed Imogen for the job. She was the opposite of her husband: warm, friendly, most of all transparently genuine. She was also the opposite of her son in a way. She was dark-haired and brown-eyed. Her complexion was almost Mediterranean.

'How was your first day?' she asked.

'Fine,' said Imogen. But she couldn't hide the bad taste her encounter with The Boys had left.

'Sure?'

'Well, The Boys did tease me a bit.'

'The Boys?' said Mrs Hewlett. 'You must have been listening to Barry.'

Imogen nodded. 'We did have a chat. He wants me to be nice to them.'

'I wouldn't be *too* nice,' Mrs Hewlett advised. 'Middle-aged men away from home and all that. Anyway, you seem to have done a good job.' She smiled. 'I knew you would.'

Imogen returned the smile. 'Thanks.'

'Oh, before you go, I know who you haven't met – my son.'

'Anthony,' said Imogen. 'Your husband introduced us.'

Mrs Hewlett looked surprised, but she recovered herself.

'Well, that's about it. You get off home, Imogen. You know when you're due back here?'

'Yes,' said Imogen. 'Half-past four. To help get the evening meals ready.'

'Good girl.'

Imogen took off her apron and walked down the corridor to the back door. As she stepped out into the July heat, she became aware of a presence – white, almost colourless.

Anthony.

I enjoyed shooting her. Does that shock you? Or maybe you've rumbled me. Sussed my little joke, have you? Aren't you the sharp one! That's right, I shot her through a photo lens. When my dad, my natural father the scumbag, walked out on Mum and me, you know what he left me? A black eye and a second-hand camera. The black eye was on purpose. The Pentax was an oversight.

*

Anthony watched Imogen turn right on to Old Lane and walk towards Mill Street. He already knew where she lived – that four-bedroomed detached on the Kiddington Road. He'd looked up the address the day she came for interview. He'd sneaked her letter of application out of Barry's file.

Anthony wondered why she needed a job in this dump. Her family couldn't be short of a bob or two, living over on that side of the village. OK, so they'd probably bought the house when property prices were cheaper, but there was never a time when anything on the Kiddington Road went for a song. No, Imogen must want the job for reasons of her own.

Anthony craned to see her as she reached the corner. She intrigued him.

At the junction with Marsham Lane Imogen waited for a car to pass. It would be Anthony's last glimpse of her until late that afternoon. He savoured it. His pupils seemed to jump more than usual. His blue, restless eyes lit with a strange flame. He liked to look at her. If only she were closer! She was wearing a sleeveless white top and a tan skirt. Her suntanned legs were bare. No tights. Her skin shone.

Anthony followed her movements as she jogged across Marsham Lane, then slowed and carried on towards the High Street. She walked with an easy rhythm, hair swaying down her slender back. How he would love to touch that hair – that rich, honey-blonde hair! Anthony watched her as far as he could down Old Lane and into Mill Street.

When she had gone he slowly, regretfully, closed the door.

Here she is – Imogen, my Imogen. It's a good shot, if I say so myself. I took it with the long lens, through the open window to the breakfast room. See the way her hair falls? See the way the girl-freckles nestle in the neckline of her top? You can understand why I fell in love with her the way I did.

This is the one good thing about Mum marrying that fat fool Barry – I get this great en suite dark room. Too big to be a cupboard, too small to be a separate room, I can't imagine what it was used for in the old days. Maybe this is where they locked up the mad relatives, the oddballs, people like me. The main thing is, it's here. This is where I develop my pictures after I've shot them. Every cloud has a silver lining, you see. My stinking father walks out, he leaves the Pentax. Lousy, porky Barry shacks up with my mum, I get my own dark room.

Silver linings.

Then Barry decides to take on somebody casual over the summer months. Incredible, isn't it? Barry, with his fat-guy pants and his pathetic permed dog, he actually did something right. He found Imogen.

The best silver lining of the lot.

Because she's the one I love, and I get to shoot her.

NO PLACE FOR ASYLUM SEEKERS

Villagers whose land borders a foot-and-mouth burial pit say their village is being used as a dumping ground.

John and Muriel Thompson's back garden is just 200m away from the burial pit on Crofton Road, and now the area could become home to hundreds of asylum seekers.

The couple are furious at plans to build a detention centre on their doorstep.

'First it's animal carcases,' said Mrs Thompson, 'now it's asylum seekers. It's the wrong place for these people. There's no bus service, no train service, and nothing for them to do. There's 100,000 dead bodies out the back.

We don't need a few hundred live ones.'

As many as 600 people could be housed at the site.

'We're not anti-refugee,' Mr Green said, 'but why here?'

Mr Green was of the opinion that Marsham would be spoiled by the influx.

'They're going to ruin an area of natural beauty,' said the 55-year-old.

Councillor Bob Thetford said, 'The Government says it wants to disperse refugees across the country. It is a mistaken policy. This is too big a burden for a small rural community. We won't take this lying down.'

Two

I spy with my little eye, something beginning with I.

Imogen saw the second-floor curtains twitch from halfway along Old Lane. She knew who it was – Anthony. The Hewletts' accommodation was on the top floor of Old Marsham Inn. Glimpsing the ghost-face at the window, she gave a cheery wave. He didn't return the greeting.

'You're early,' said Barry Hewlett, meeting her in the dining-room doorway.

'Only ten minutes,' said Imogen, glancing at her watch.

'Don't apologise,' he told her. 'It's good to see.'

Hewlett turned and crossed the dining room. Imogen watched him putting the evening menus into small plastic holders. He reminded her of Basil Fawlty, only shorter and fatter and a dog-lover. The poodle guy. What a saddo!

'Imogen,' he called, 'would you mind putting out the cutlery?'

She got to the arch separating the kitchen from the dining room.

'And don't forget to wrap it in napkins.'

'Napkins?' Imogen said.

'Napkins.'

Imogen pulled a handful of red napkins from the drawer and headed for the tables.

'Apron,' Hewlett said. 'Always wear the appropriate clothing.'

Imogen nodded, made herself *appropriate*, and returned.

'There,' said Hewlett. 'That's better. Got to keep the customer satisfied.'

Imogen pulled a face then watched him waddle back into the kitchen followed by Trixie, wondering how exactly a handful of red napkins and a stupid white apron kept the customer satisfied. Still, she thought, ours is not to reason why, ours is just to do and fry. The final rhyme popped into her mind as she heard the gammon steaks sizzling in the pan.

She just waved at me.

At me!

Until this moment she was an image, a doll on a pedestal. She's the most beautiful creature I've ever seen. There was no chance with Imogen, not for somebody like me.

It isn't just the way I look either – the eye-flicker, the whiteness of me. No, it isn't that that sets me apart. There are plenty of kids who handle it just fine. It isn't a physical thing at all. With me, the freak is inside. Maybe my lousy dad put it there. Maybe it was there all the time. All I know is, all my life girls have been a race apart. I just can't think what to say to them. I get tongue-tied. That's the whole point about me. I don't get to know people.

I shoot them.

It was the moment Imogen had been dreading. Oh puke! The Boys had just come in together. But there was no sign of The Professor. What was his name again? Yes, Craig. Sad, balding, nerdy Gordon Craig was nowhere to be seen.

'Where's Mr Craig?' Imogen asked, making an effort.

'Doing his *Times* crossword, I shouldn't wonder,' Wise told her. 'He'll be down. Likes his afters, does The Professor. Partial to a bit of cheesecake.'

They had changed out of their workclothes. They were dressed in jeans and T-shirts. Riley's bore the slogan *Drink Till You Drop*, signalling his intentions for the rest of the evening.

'Can I take your order?' Imogen asked.

'We'll wait for The Professor,' Wise said.

'You can bring us two lagers though,' said Riley, 'and a shandy for the Prof.'

'Well said, Scouse,' Wise commented approvingly.

Imogen glanced at Hewlett. She wasn't sure how she stood about going into the bar. She was, after all, only just turned sixteen.

'That's all right, Imogen,' said Hewlett, appearing from nowhere. 'I'll sort out the drinks. You see to The Boys.'

'Much appreciated,' said Wise. 'I like being seen to by a pretty girl.'

Imogen blushed.

'Eh, slow down there, Mickey,' said Riley, grinning broadly. 'She's only sixteen, isn't that right, Im?'

She wanted to take the lagers when they came and pour them over the men's heads.

My name isn't Im, you moron, it's Imogen.

In the event, a new arrival saved her the time and effort.

'Stop teasing the girl,' said Craig, taking his place at the table. 'You especially, Mickey. You should know better. You've got a daughter her age.'

For the first time somebody had stopped Wise in his tracks. The smile crumpled from his face.

'I was only joking, Gordon.'

That Craig had brought his workmates to heel was obvious. Suddenly he was Craig rather than The Professor.

'So are you ready to order?' Imogen asked, recovering her composure.

'Ready as we'll ever be,' chirped Riley. 'I could eat a scabby horse between two bread vans.'

Wise grinned. 'And leave the saddles on.'

Imogen gave Wise her forced smile. Finally they were ready to order.

This is the gallery.

I've got them all here: Mum, Barry, The Boys, the other staff and most of the villagers. And now Imogen. Sweet Imogen. I look at my photographs blu-tacked to the wall and I feel good. I can't say I usually like the real thing, flesh-and-blood 3-D people. They're cruel, they hurt you just for fun, and they're pushy. They fill the space around me, shrinking me, fading me out until I'm almost invisible.

But when I shoot them, I'm the one who fills the space and they're the ones who shrink.

Then there's you, my lovely Imogen, the one exception. You're dream and reality in one. I know you'll never hurt me. You're my new start.

The Boys were ready to order dessert.

'What'll it be, Professor?' Wise asked.

'Got to be cheesecake,' said Riley.

He caught Imogen's eye.

'Gordon does like his cheesecake.'

Imogen had the distinct feeling that tiny insects were running over her skin. Craig ignored them. He was staring at a book, though Imogen knew he wasn't reading. The book was a protection, something on which to fix his gaze so he could blot out their inane chatter.

'What are you reading, Mr Craig?' she asked.

Craig showed her the cover. It was *To Kill A Mockingbird.*

'It's a wonderful book,' she said.

His face flooded with pleasure.

'You've read it?'

Imogen met his surprised look.

'Mum says I'm like Scout Finch. I was born reading.'

Craig glanced at his workmates.

'That's not a bad thing,' he said.

'I think The Professor's telling us off,' said Wise. 'No time for the common herd, have you, Gordon?'

'I've no time for ignorance,' said Craig tetchily.

'So what's your order?' Imogen asked, not liking the course the conversation was taking.

'Apple pie,' said Wise.

'Make that two,' said Riley.

'And,' Wise chuckled, winking at Imogen, 'cheesecake for The Professor.'

But Craig stood up abruptly. Crockery rattled and milk slopped on to the tablecloth.

'No dessert for me,' he snapped. 'I'm going to read in the lounge.'

His workmates watched him go, amused looks on their faces.

'Well,' said Wise. 'What's the matter with The Prof? Was it something I said?'

I could watch her all night.

Look at her – so lovely, so graceful. She doesn't mind being seen with me. Though I hardly dare say it, I think she might even like me. I've put her photographs right at the centre of my gallery. She is the sun and the rest of us, like planets, orbit around her.

She is the centre of my universe.

'Hello,' said Wise, rocking back on his chair and looking at the arch. 'Who's this?'

Anthony tried to dart back out of sight.

'Well, if it isn't our Goz!'

Imogen was bringing their coffee.

'Goz?' she said. 'Why do you call him that?'

Wise laughed. 'Gozzy,' he explained. He crossed his eyes.

'I think that's cruel,' Imogen said.

This time she didn't care what Barry Hewlett thought.
She wasn't going to let the comment pass. Wise ignored
her. He was moving his eyes, imitating the nystagmus.

'Oh, come on, sweet cakes,' said Riley. 'We're only
having a laugh.'

He called over to Anthony. 'You don't mind, do you,
Gozzy lad?'

Anthony stayed out of sight, not saying a word. It was
left to Imogen to fight his battles for him.

'I still don't think you should talk to him like that. He's
got a name – Anthony.'

With that, she spun round on her heel and marched
away. Behind her, The Boys made their feelings known.

'Oo-ooh!' Wise and Riley chorused. 'Touchy, isn't she?'

Did you hear that?

*She stood up for me! Imogen stopped their teasing, and
she did it for me.*

For me!

There was no comeback. The Boys didn't complain about
Imogen. They enjoyed winding her up. Barry Hewlett was
none the wiser. In fact, when he caught up with Imogen
half an hour later, he was positively beaming. Even Trixie
looked happy.

'I can see you're an asset already,' he said. 'It's just a pity
you'll be going back to school. I could do with somebody
like you on my permanent staff. You wouldn't consider it,
I don't suppose?'

Sure! thought Imogen. I'd really enjoy wasting my life round this dump! She didn't say that, of course.

'Sorry, Mr Hewlett,' she said, 'I'll be too busy. I want to go to university.'

'Pity,' said Hewlett. 'What are you going to study?'

'English, maybe combined with French. Literature's always been my thing.'

'I'm not much of a reader myself,' Hewlett said. 'Too much to do. I pick up the odd Jeffrey Archer, that's all. Ever read him?'

Imogen shook her head. She didn't want to either!

'Well, good luck to you, Imogen,' said Hewlett. 'I could do with more like you. See you tomorrow.'

Imogen managed a smile. 'Bye, Mr Hewlett.'

She made for the door. It was propped open by a wooden wedge and cool air met her at the threshold. The day's heat was relaxing its grip a little and evening breezes were eddying through the woods. Imogen raised her face to meet the freshness. She closed her eyes and dusk gathered in her mind. When she opened her eyes again Anthony was there. She gave a startled yelp.

'Sorry,' he said hurriedly. 'I didn't mean to scare you.'

Imogen giggled self-consciously. 'That's all right,' she said. 'I shouldn't be so jumpy.'

'No,' said Anthony. 'I like it. You're like a little bird.'

Her hazel eyes met his.

'Anthony, what a funny thing to say!'

'Have I offended you?'

'No,' she said. 'It's unusual, that's all.'

'Good unusual or bad unusual?'

Imogen smiled. He watched her full lips.

'I don't know, just unusual.'

Anthony frowned.

'Barry's always calling me odd.'

He fingered his glasses.

'Do you think I'm odd?'

The honest answer would have been yes.

'I don't know you that well,' Imogen said.

It was a weak reply, but honest as far as it went.

'Sensitive maybe. That isn't a bad thing.'

The word sensitive seemed to encourage him.

'I read poetry.'

He waited a beat then added, 'Love poetry.'

Anthony looked at her, as if expecting her to say something. When she didn't, he seemed disappointed.

'Anyway,' Anthony said, 'thanks, for what you said earlier.'

'It was nothing.'

Anthony shook his head fiercely.

'No,' he said, contradicting her. 'Nobody has ever stood up for me like that. It was something, all right.'

'They're ignorant,' she said. 'They don't know any better. Does it bother you? Your . . .'

Imogen frowned. What was she going to call it? His disability, his problem, his syndrome? She settled for . . . 'condition.'

'Not really,' he said. 'Though my eyesight isn't that great.'

Imogen sensed there was something more.

'And?'

'And I get bullied.'

Imogen thought of Wise.

'What sort of bullying?'

'Name-calling, kids pulling faces at me, pushing and shoving – you know the kind of thing.'

'That's awful! Doesn't your school do anything about it?'

Anthony shook his head.

'I had to sort it myself.'

He grinned.

'I gave a kid a bloody nose.'

'You did!'

Imogen thought he might be making it up. After all, he was no Jean-Claude Van Damme.

'Where do you go?' she asked.

'Kiddington High. You?'

'Mount Carmel School for Girls. The teachers really don't do anything about the bullying?'

'No,' said Anthony. 'They've got plenty of policies and all that – you could paper the walls with them – but they don't mean a thing. The truth is, the teachers think I bring it on myself. They even blamed me for fighting back. That's why it's great that you stood up for me.'

'Honestly,' she said, 'it's nothing.'

Which, to Imogen, was exactly what it was – nothing, a small, soon-forgotten attempt to stand up for fair play. On impulse, she gave him a peck on the cheek.

'See you tomorrow, Anthony.'

He watched her all the way down the Lane, until she was out of sight. When she was gone he touched his cheek. There, her kiss still burned.

Rewind.

School, two weeks ago. Actually, the teachers did do something about the bullying.

They put the blame on me.

It goes like this. I'm coming out of the canteen. Three boys are waiting for me. I feel a shudder of apprehension. The ringleaders are both there: Jamie Smith and Paul Jones. Around school, they're affectionately known as Alias Smith and Jones. But I've no affection for them. To most people they're good guys, to me they're hell on legs. The moment they see me, they start. 'Hey, here's Albie!'

Original, eh? They call me Albie No. Paul Jones stands in my way and starts jumping to and fro in front of me.

'If I go fast enough, do you think you could keep your eyes on me?' he says.

I try to shove past. Now he's waggling his head from side to side.

'This fast enough, Albie? Can you see me now?'

I tell him to leave me alone.

But they don't know the meaning of the word. All the way down the corridor I can hear their voices.

'Albie No! Albie No!'

'That you, Imogen?'

'Yes, Mum.'

Mum met her in the hallway.

'I thought I might have to leave you a note,' she said. 'Your dad and I are going into Crofton.'

'Crofton? How come?'

'There's a meeting at the village hall, about the proposal to build this detention centre.'

The Bayliss family would be in a minority, probably of three. The odds appealed to Imogen. We few, we happy few!

'Can I come?'

Mum looked doubtful.

'It might get a bit heated. Tempers are starting to get frayed.'

'Mum,' Imogen reminded her mother, 'I'm a big girl now.'

Dad came down the stairs.

'What do you think, Tim?' Mum said.

'Let her come, Karen,' he said. 'She's been in hairier situations than a village meeting. Remember the bypass campaign? She was with us when we stood in the way of that earth-mover.'

'OK,' said Mum, 'but we've got to go in two minutes. Make yourself a sandwich quickly.'

'That's OK, Mum,' said Imogen. 'I had a pasta salad at work.'

She liked the sound of that. 'Work.' It made her feel as though she had crossed a threshold somehow.

'The Hewletts are feeding you then?' said Dad. 'That's good.'

'Right,' said Mum. 'Let's make a move. We want a good seat.'

'Oh, I know you,' said Dad. 'You just want to catch the eye of the Chair first.'

'Too right,' said Mum. 'We need to get our two-pennyworth in before the bigots.'

'Now, now,' said Dad. 'If you go expecting bigots that's exactly what you'll get. Try to keep an open mind.'

Dad had always been the ice to his wife's fire.

'Mmm,' said Mum. 'Keep an open mind? That's more than they'll do.'

Imogen followed her parents out to the car.

Rewind.

Three days later.

Paul Jones greets me wearing a pair of joke glasses, painted ping-pong balls on springs. The pupils ooze from the glasses, bouncing and colliding.

'Oh no!' Jones is groaning. 'I've caught it off you, Albie. I've got wonky eye-tis.'

Smith and two other lads are roaring fit to burst, forcing out laughter like toothpaste from the tube.

'Get out of my way,' I tell them.

But Jones is having too much fun humiliating me. By now he's skipping from one foot to the other, the ping-pong eyes weaving crazy patterns in front of his face.

'Help me, Albie! Do something, will you? There's got to be something you can do for me.'

I try to sidestep him, but he grabs my sleeve. He's

clinging on. That's when I do it. I pull back my elbow and slam it into his face. There's a satisfying crunch as his nose breaks, then Jones is screaming.

I watch the thin, scarlet blood exploding over his white shirt.

I've done something for him.

From Marsham it is only two miles to Crofton, but nobody in their right mind would walk from one village to the other. There is no pavement on the winding B road, not even a grass verge to speak of, and only the most foolhardy pedestrian would brave the many speeding vehicles. In this neck of the woods BMW Man rules supreme. When the Baylisses arrived in Crofton, they had to drive round the village three times before they could find a single parking space.

'Big turnout,' said Dad.

He sounded apprehensive. He wasn't a born fighter like his wife. He was right about the numbers going to the meeting. Cars clogged the picturesque lanes just off the village green, their near-side wheels pulled up on the pavements.

'Looks like the green welly brigade are really wound up over this one,' said Mum, scowling at the Countryside Alliance stickers in the windows of several vehicles.

Imogen followed her parents into the Parish Hall, where they were forced to stand at the back. She was starting to wonder why she hadn't stayed at home.

'So much for setting off early,' said Mum.

'It's a pity they couldn't keep Marsham Parish Hall going,' Dad said. 'It's twice the size of this one.'

Marsham Parish Hall had been boarded up the previous summer, originally for repairs to storm damage. The repairs had never happened, constantly postponed for lack of funding.

A strawberry-nosed man next to the Baylisses overheard them.

'Terrible, the way things are going,' he said. 'First the Post Office, then the Parish Hall. It'll be the pub next.'

He took their silence as agreement.

'Might as well shut the countryside altogether.'

Rewind.

The day after the elbow.

Mum and I in Mr Latham's office. I let the discussion over my future swirl round me like cigarette smoke. I do my best not to inhale.

'. . . obvious provocation, anti-swot culture at the bottom of it. But not the way to deal with it. Can't condone violence . . .'

'. . . not like him. Such a quiet boy usually . . .'

'. . . first incident of its type, but very serious. Nose broken. Parents up in arms . . .'

'. . . really worried it will harm his school career. He's so bright. Should be some consideration for the gifted and talented pupil . . .'

'. . . suspension until the end of the academic year. Give everyone a breathing space. Time to reflect . . .'

But as I walk out of Mr Latham's office, I don't feel punished. I feel liberated. *Exhilaration floods through me. I can look forward to six whole weeks free of Smith and Jones.*

No girls with flowing hair and glowing skin to remind me what I can't touch, can't kiss.

Nobody except the specimens I shoot.

In Crofton Parish Hall the temperature was rising, and not just because of the press of bodies on a hot July evening. Imogen had been getting bored, texting her best friend Katie, when a woman in her early twenties, introducing herself as a member of the Kiddington Refugee

Committee, launched a passionate defence of the right of asylum seekers to live in the area. On only one issue did she win the support of the majority of the audience.

'Like you,' she said, 'I am against a detention centre.'

She was interrupted by applause, but waved it impatiently away. She wasn't the sort to court popularity.

'But,' she added, 'it is definitely not because I am opposed to refugees settling in the area.'

Imogen liked the look of the speaker. For a few moments she was drowned out by a barrage of catcalls and protests. *So where are you from?* she was asked. *Another outsider, I'll bet.* None of it fazed her.

'No,' she persisted, refusing to rise to the bait, 'I am opposed to the centre because it is a prison in all but name. Refugees are not criminals.'

The statement caused uproar but she struggled on.

'They deserve decent housing and the chance to earn a living like the rest of us.'

Strawberry Nose was halfway through shouting something about the burden on the Welfare State when he noticed the Baylisses applauding the speaker.

'You're not trying to tell me you think we should take them in?' he gasped, appalled.

'I think,' Mum replied, 'that asylum seekers should be allowed to settle wherever they wish. Locking them up is a very poor solution to the problem.'

'Sending them back's better,' snapped Strawberry Nose, demonstrating his disgust by moving away.

After half a dozen hostile contributions, each more loudly applauded than the last, Mum managed to get herself noticed by the Chair.

'Thank you,' she said. 'I would like to support the young woman from the Kiddington Refugee group.'

She was met by loud groans. 'Another flipping do-gooder!' was one of the more polite.

'Sanctuary,' Mum struggled on, 'is an age-old tradition in this country . . .'

Her words were greeted with a Quasimodo impression. 'Thanctuary, Ethmerelda! Thanctuary!'

'Yes, very funny,' said Mum, utterly po-faced. 'The point is, these people are genuine refugees . . .'

Shouts of *Rubbish!* An elderly woman waved the *Marsham Observer* article about the proposed site in her face.

'As I understand it,' Mum ploughed on, 'there are a small number of asylum seekers staying in bed and breakfast accommodation in Kiddington.'

Nods from the woman from the Refugee Committee.

'What they need is a proper home, the chance to earn a living and . . .' By now her voice could hardly be heard, 'And a proper welcome from local people.'

'Well, they can whistle for that,' somebody shouted to loud laughter.

When Mum finally struggled to the end of her speech she was received with loud applause by half a dozen people and impatient heckling by the remaining hundred or so.

I like it here in my room.

The ceiling is irregular and sloping, like a poet's garret. I can imagine Byron or Shelley sitting here. The sounds of the bar are muffled. Ignorant voices fade to a low rumble. This is as close to peace as I have ever been in my life. At the moment I am reading Birdsong *by Sebastian Faulks. I read how the main character Stephen falls in love with his Isabelle. It makes me think of Imogen.*

My Imogen.

That's when I notice the birdsong outside my window.

Life is good. It doesn't have to hurt.

Mum had just pressed the key fob to de-activate the car

alarm and they were about to get in when they heard a voice.

'Excuse me!' It was the woman from the Refugee committee.

'Hi, my name is Sophie Hart. I wanted to thank you for your support in there.'

'It didn't do an awful lot of good, did it?' Mum said. 'I'm turning into the patron saint of lost causes.'

'No,' said Sophie, 'it's going to be an uphill struggle.'

Sophie looked every bit the campaign activist. She was wearing motorcycle leathers and she had a nose stud. Imogen smiled to herself. There was a time two years ago when she'd wanted one herself. Her parents had said no. Long-time lefties they might be, but they weren't having their little girl looking like *that*!

'If you're interested,' Sophie said, 'we have regular meetings at Kiddington Law Centre.'

Imogen was the first to answer.

'What do you do?' she asked.

'Oh, keep in contact with the asylum seekers, arrange advice, that kind of thing. A lot of them are very isolated. This dispersal idea creates a lot of problems, driving them away from the communities in the big cities. Then there's the question of representing them in appeals. Believe me, there's always plenty to do.'

Sophie handed Imogen a card. Asserting her prerogative as a parent, Mum took it.

Imogen wanted to snatch it back but it wasn't worth getting grounded. Katie would be calling to go out sometime this week. There was no sense in ruining it for herself.

'We'll think about it,' Mum said – a little frostily, Imogen thought.

She was disappointed at Mum's reaction. More and more, she heard them say they'd *done their bit*.

By way of compensation for their lukewarm response,

Imogen said: 'I'll see if I can get along. I've got a job until seven, you see, and no transport.'

Sophie pointed out a tall man, also in his early twenties. He was standing by a Suzuki motorbike.

'I'm sure Kes would pick you up.'

Mum darted Imogen a glance that said: *You're getting on that contraption over my dead body!*

'What does Kes stand for?' Imogen asked.

'Dunno,' said Sophie. 'To be honest, I've never asked.' She laughed. 'He's my boyfriend. He's just Kes.'

She pulled on her helmet.

'Anyway, we've got to be going. Thanks again. I do hope you can get along to a meeting.'

The Baylisses smiled, Mum and Dad non-committally, Imogen broadly.

Three

'Eager to get away, are you?'

Imogen turned towards the speaker. It was Mickey Wise. Three days after the meeting at Crofton Parish Hall, she had more on her mind.

'I beg your pardon?'

'You were miles away,' said Peter Riley.

Imogen was aware of their eyes on her, and Gordon Craig, like a trusty guard dog, keeping a close watch on their behaviour. She flashed him a smile. It was almost as if he had adopted her – her unofficial uncle.

'Meeting somebody after work?' asked Wise.

'Boyfriend?' asked Riley.

'No,' said Imogen, flesh starting to crawl. 'Nothing like that.'

Her tone of voice signalled that she'd said quite enough. She cleared the dessert dishes and took them into the kitchen.

'Are you all right?' asked Mrs Hewlett, busy with the washing up.

'Yes. Why do you ask?'

'You don't seem to have your mind on the job this evening. You've taken meals to the wrong table twice. It's not like you, Imogen. I wondered if something was bothering you.'

'I'm getting a lift into Kiddington,' Imogen told her. 'I don't want to miss it.'

Mrs Hewlett leaned forward, as if sharing a confidence. 'Something exciting?'

'Not really, just something I've got to do.'

Mrs Hewlett glanced at the clock.

'What time are you getting picked up?'

'Ten past seven, in the High Street.'

'Why don't you go at five to?' Mrs Hewlett asked. 'Then you'll be sure to get there on time.'

Imogen beamed.

'You wouldn't mind?'

'What's five minutes? I can manage here.'

'And Mr Hewlett, what will he say?'

Mrs Hewlett's dark features creased with a conspiratorial smile.

'Don't worry about Barry. He's upstairs feeling sorry for himself.' She rolled her eyes. 'He's coming down with a summer cold. You know what men are like. Don't worry about old Grumpy Bear – I'll square it with him.'

So it was that, at five past seven, Imogen was waiting by the bowling green on the High Street. She was feeling self-conscious. What do you wear to a Refugee Committee meeting, anyway? First she'd gone for the grungey look, all shapeless tops and baggy jeans, but it wasn't very flattering. Then she'd got dressed up, black trousers and a crisp white top, but that struck her as a bit much for an hour and a half in a Law Centre. Finally she'd settled for denim skirt and hooded mesh vest. Neutral, basically.

She was still twitching at the hem of her skirt when she heard the throb of an engine and looked up expectantly. It wasn't Kes's motorbike but an ancient, pale green car. To Imogen's surprise, it pulled into the kerb.

'Do you need a lift anywhere?' the driver asked.

'Oh, it's you, Mr Craig,' Imogen said.

She was surprised. When she left he had only just started drinking his coffee. The guy must have an asbestos throat. She looked at the car.

'Is this yours?'

'Yes,' Craig said. 'Hillman Imp. It takes me back to my wasted youth.'

Imogen stifled a laugh. Surely a wasted youth demanded something more powerful than this little runabout? It was only one step up from a Robin Reliant.

'I restored it myself,' Craig continued. 'Poor old thing was mouldering in a scrap yard.'

'You've done a great job,' Imogen said.

'Thanks. So, do you need that lift?'

'That's very kind, but I'm waiting for someone.'

Cue Kes turning off the Kiddington Road. Craig watched the bike approach, then nodded and pulled away.

'Who was that?' Kes asked.

'A guest where I work,' Imogen replied. 'Nice guy.'

Kes handed her a helmet.

'Put this on. I'm under orders from your mum to take it easy.'

Imogen wrinkled her nose.

'It's a wonder she isn't round here somewhere, spying on me,' she said.

But it wasn't Mum who was watching Imogen climb on to Kes's bike.

It was Anthony.

What are you doing, Imogen?

I didn't see you as a biker's chick. I mean, it's so Nineteen Seventies. Don't you understand what you've done? You've broken my heart. Bit of a cliché, I know, but that's just how it feels. It's as if somebody has reached in my chest, cracked open my ribs and ripped my heart in two. How could you make me think you cared, then do this? It's not fair.

34

This isn't my Imogen.

The numbers at the Refugee Committee meeting were disappointing – just ten people, and that included Imogen. Sophie Hart was obviously the driving force. She introduced every item on the agenda.

'Kiddington Mosque has taken on most of the responsibilities for welfare,' she said, 'seeing as the majority of asylum seekers locally are Muslims. That leaves us free to concentrate on campaigning. Sir Richard Gill—'

She was interrupted.

'Who's he?' asked an angry-looking teenager in a combat jacket. He appeared to have only one eyebrow. He had sat through the meeting, arms crossed belligerently, looking more and more angry.

'Sir Richard Gill,' Sophie said patiently, 'is the local MP.'

Her explanation was greeted with a loud grunt.

'Yes, Andy,' Sophie continued, 'I know you don't think much of Parliament but Sir Richard attracts the press. There are two events coming up. He's speaking at the Town Hall, then there's his regular surgery. I suggest that as many of us as possible go along to get our point of view across.'

She handed out details of both venues.

'What's the point?' said Angry Andy.

His frown unsettled Imogen. With only one brow to beetle he looked unbalanced somehow. She was starting to wonder what she was doing here.

'What's his problem?' she whispered to Kes.

'Andy? He's an anarchist,' Kes explained.

'Oh.'

Imogen didn't know much about anarchists – didn't they have something to do with Batman cloaks and bombs like painted black balloons? – but she accepted the explanation.

When Sophie had wound up the meeting, she asked Imogen what she thought.

'Oh, it was . . . interesting.'

'You mean boring, don't you?'

Imogen hesitated a beat, then admitted it. 'A bit.'

'I thought so too,' said Sophie.

'You did?'

'Sure. People think running a campaign is all marches and lobbies. It takes a lot of work behind the scenes to change people's minds. For every high-profile event, there are many evenings of boring leg work.'

Imogen nodded. 'I can see that.'

'Plus you attract some real oddballs.'

Imogen thought of Angry Andy. 'I can see that too.'

They laughed.

'I'd better give you a lift back,' said Kes. 'We don't want your parents getting worried.'

But as Imogen followed Kes to the bike, she saw a familiar car. Her heart sank.

'Dad?' she said. 'What are you doing here?'

'Your mum sent me,' Dad said. 'She didn't want you coming back by motorbike. Not in the dark.'

He glanced at Kes. 'No offence.'

'None taken,' said Kes, laid-back as ever. 'It saves me a run.'

This is my favourite shot of you, Imogen.

I took it the very first time I saw you, through the dining-room window. Your head is leaning forward, your dark-blonde hair falling over your face. You look so shy, so innocent. But you're not, are you? Well, go off with your biker friend. See if I care.

But that's the problem, Imogen.

I do.

I care so much.

36

Anthony was walking by New Pool. The August heat puddled around him and the promise of pain to come shimmered in the twilit world. He had been walking the lanes around Marsham ever since he saw Imogen climb on the back of the motorbike. Here, on the southern edge of the village where Slaughter Lane dissected Hawkstone Pool and New Pool and the river Medlon babbled under a stone bridge, he could be what he wanted to be – a ghost haunting the outer limits of time. Modern-day life seemed to have retreated over the horizon, leaving what was eternal in the English countryside. Anthony stood on an old lane with a strip of grass down the middle, alone with his thoughts.

He pulled out the photograph of Imogen, the one he had taken that first time in the dining room, and looked at it long and hard. For a moment his face hardened, and it seemed as if he would tear it in half, then he stopped and put it back in his jacket pocket. With a shrug of his shoulders he turned for home.

Two minutes away from Old Marsham Inn he made a decision. He would cross the road to avoid being seen and carry on up Old Lane into the village. There he would wait for Imogen to return.

By the time Anthony had reached the High Street a faint night wind had started to rise, struggling against the oppressive heat. Up ahead streetlights were starting to glitter like fireflies dancing in the dark. He was being drawn back to modern life, to the confusion and the cruelty where he didn't really belong. But Imogen was there, his Imogen, and if that was where she moved that was where he had to be.

At the junction of High Street and Kiddington Road, Anthony started his vigil. Far off, beyond Kiddington, the grey sea boomed and twilight passed into night.

*

Eight miles away in Kiddington three men were also walking in the twilight. They were Afghans, brought here by war, by fear and need. The youngest, Farid, followed his friends Hamid and Ahmed back to the Carnforth House Hotel, a slowly disintegrating premises which had been their home for the last six months.

'Hey, Farid!' Hamid shouted. 'Race you back.'

Hamid and Ahmed set off down the street. Farid chased after them. They were close to the hotel when an elderly couple saw them coming and crossed the road. Farid, who had almost caught up with the others, forgot about the horseplay. He stopped and stared after them. What made these two old people so afraid of him and his friends?

'Hey Farid, what have you stopped for?'

'Did you see that?'

'What?'

'The way they crossed the road to avoid us.'

'Forget it,' Ahmed told him. 'It happens all the time. So what?'

Farid wasn't about to forget it. 'But we weren't doing anything.'

'We don't have to,' said Hamid. 'Just being here is enough.'

Farid let the thought hang for a moment, wondering how long he had, then followed his friends.

Carnforth House was a guest house on Marsham Road. Forty years earlier it had been at the hub of a brisk holiday trade, but now all that had been attracted abroad. Holiday-makers had been replaced by social security claimants and asylum seekers. Long gone was the cheery welcome of the seaside hotelier, replaced by a weary nostalgia for the good old days.

'Do you want to play pool?' Hamid asked.

Farid shook his head. The thought of being flown back

to Germany, his last stop-over before Britain, haunted him. Was it too much to expect a future?

'No, I'm tired. I'm going to bed.'

Imogen got out of the car and stamped into the house.

'That was so embarrassing!' she said, confronting Mum. 'What were you thinking of? I already had a lift.'

'I wasn't going to have you come home on that motorbike,' said Mum.

'A couple of years and you won't be able to stop me,' said Imogen.

'That's right,' said Mum, '*a couple of years*. Until then, we set the rules.'

'You're impossible,' said Imogen, heading for the stairs.

'If you think you're going off in a huff,' Mum said, 'you've got another think coming.'

Imogen was still thinking of an answer when Mum came back.

'Katie called earlier about going out. You'll sit down, calm down, and ask politely, otherwise you don't go at all. Is that understood?'

Imogen mumbled something.

'I said: is that understood?'

Imogen sighed. 'Yes, Mum.'

Brought home by Daddy, were you? Now, that's encouraging. So what gives? Maybe all is not lost. There's hope, after all. Could there be an innocent explanation for going off with the biker? I stand out on the road, watching lights go on. Which room is yours, Imogen? I try to imagine the warm world behind the curtains. What are you talking about, in there with your parents, and what do you dream about alone in your room?

I wish it was me.

*

Imogen lay on her stomach on the bed, ankles crossed, as she talked to Katie.

'You don't know how lucky you are,' she told Katie. 'The wrinklies are always on my case.'

After a row, Mum and Dad were always the wrinklies.

'So where were you tonight?' Katie asked.

'The Refugee Committee.'

'Oh no, don't tell me you're going to go all earnest on me! You're not going to start wearing badges again?'

'Might do.'

Katie made a finger-down-the-throat noise.

'Girl, you're sixteen. You want to have fun.'

'Boys aren't the only way of having fun,' said Imogen.

'Tell me a better way,' said Katie. 'Now, talking of boys . . .'

When Anthony reached the Old Marsham Inn he let himself in the back way. The heat, cigarette smoke and laughter from the bar hit him like the blast from an oven. A slimy nausea took hold of him and he jogged up the stairs past the guest rooms to the second floor.

He paused at the living-room door. Mum and Barry were lying on the couch. She had her back against his chest and he was stroking the back of her leg with his foot. Anthony watched in disgust while the stockinged toe rubbed his mother's calf as if to say: 'I own you.' The way that proprietorial toe wiggled – it just made him sick. It reminded him of something he had read in *Women in Love* by D.H. Lawrence: 'The world all in couples, each couple in its own little house, watching its own little interests and stewing in its own little privacy – it's the most repulsive thing on earth.'

Anthony watched Mum and Barry.

Repulsive.

Mum must have become aware of his presence because she called to him.

'Is that you, Anthony?'

'Yes.'

'Why don't you come in and sit down? There's a really good film on TV.'

Anthony grimaced. Barry was still nursing his head cold. He smelled of extra-strong mints and Olbas Oil. He had been sucking the mints constantly for two days and always had a few drops of Olbas Oil on his handkerchief. It was a good idea to stay downwind.

'It's OK, Mum. I'm going to read.'

But Anthony didn't read. He sat in his room looking at the photograph of Imogen, the one in which she lowered her eyes and the sunlight lanced across her face.

Maybe it isn't all over.

Not yet.

LETTERS

The straw that broke the camel's back

Dear Editor,

Hear, hear! Well done, Mr and Mrs Thompson for saying what the people of Marsham and Crofton think.

We are a small rural community. The last thing we need is an influx of people of a different culture. Already we have lost our Post Office and Parish Hall.

The bus service to Kiddington has been reduced to twice a day. Don't get me wrong. I'm not racist or anti-asylum seeker, but I just don't see how we can cope with this added pressure.

I would ask readers to bombard our MP, Sir Richard Gill, with letters of protest.

Yours sincerely,
Mrs M. Atherton.

They're welcome here!

Dear Editor,

I am writing to object to the tone of last week's lead article about the proposed Crofton Detention Centre.

Asylum seekers are people just like us, fleeing war and persecution. It is not their fault that they have been 'dispersed' by the Government to areas like ours. It is time we put aside out-of-date prejudice and gave refugees a warm welcome. After all, many people who we now consider as British as bangers and mash were once refugees themselves.

Yours sincerely,
Mrs K. Bayliss

Enough is enough!

Dear Editor,

Close the gates against the flood of immigrants, that's what I say.

This country is struggling to provide for its own people, never mind thousands of so-called refugees. It is time we took up the welcome mat and said loudly: Enough is enough!

Yours faithfully,
Mr J. Hazel

Four

Imp *n.* **1.** a small devil. **2.** a mischievous child.

Next day, Friday, Imogen stood watching Gordon Craig packing the boot of his Hillman Imp. Imp? It was such a ludicrous name. Anyone less like a little devil than quiet, balding Craig was difficult to imagine. She didn't believe there was an ounce of mischief in him. It was as if somebody had hooked up a hose to him and drained him of any sense of fun. He was subdued, serious . . . and sad. He noticed her.

'Not staying for the evening meal?' she asked.

Evening meal without The Boys? Now, that would be something to look forward to!

'No,' he said. 'I won't be eating here tonight. I want to get on the road before the traffic really builds up on the motorway. The other lads have already gone. Peter's got a heck of a drive ahead of him. He'll be an hour in traffic jams in Birmingham alone.'

Heck of a drive. That was typical of Craig. He was such a gentleman he didn't even say *hell*.

'Do you like your job?' Imogen asked. 'All the travelling, staying away from home the way you do?'

Craig shrugged. 'It's a living,' he said.

43

Imogen wondered at him. You'd think he'd be happy, TGIF and all that. Instead he seemed depressed at the prospect of a weekend home. Craig threw a carrier bag into the boot after his case. The contractors finished early on Friday so they could beat the weekend traffic on the way home. He slammed the car boot.

'Got anything nice planned for the weekend?' Imogen asked, still thrown by his mood.

Come on! she beamed at him. Cheer up! The weekend starts here. She was thinking about her own evening ahead with Katie and the gang, a chance to blow off steam after a week clearing dishes.

'Anything special?'

'No, just a quiet couple of days at home with the wife.'

The wife, Imogen thought. Do people still say that?

'Children?'

Craig looked away. 'No, no children.'

Imogen had a feeling she had touched a nerve.

'Have a nice time,' she said as he slid into the driver's seat.

'Yes, you too,' he said. 'Don't do anything I wouldn't do.'

Imogen watched the pale green car pull away. That left her a lot of scope.

So what's the score, Imogen?

I can't handle this, not knowing. Are you the girl I thought you were? Or are you like all the others, swooning over some cleft chin, a pair of steely-blue eyes? I don't believe you could be so shallow. Where did you go with your biker friend? Tell me that. What did you do? Is it over, or is there still a chance for me? I just wish somehow I could bring myself to tell you how I feel.

I hate the questions that keep buzzing through my brain. I hate the uncertainty they bring. Unpleasantness, even cruelty I can endure. Misery is a routine you can learn to live with. It's like rain. Once you're soaked to the skin, you can't get any wetter. That's the thing about bullies. The likes of Smith and Jones, The Boys – they get you down, but after a while they stop hurting you.

It's hope that makes you hurt.

That's why you can still get through to me. You were my dream, Imogen. Now you're my torment.

When Craig had gone Imogen turned towards the Inn. She saw a curtain being nudged aside on the second floor.

Anthony.

With a smile, Imogen waved up at him. He didn't return the wave. She hadn't expected him to.

Anthony's strange ways didn't bother her much. She didn't find oddness at all threatening. She was used to the needy boys who stared at her from a distance. Sometimes she flashed them a smile to cheer up their sad little lives, then right away felt tight for doing it. It was leading them on, and they couldn't help being saddos. Like Dad always said, it would be a funny old world if we were all the same. Anthony was shy, that was all, and she wasn't going to cause him discomfort by pushing him to act in a way he didn't want to.

There was a spring in Imogen's step tonight. The car park was mottled with shadow and sunshine from the gnarled oaks along Old Lane. She crossed the dappled tarmac happy in the knowledge that her tormentors were sitting somewhere on the M6 or M25 in traffic jams.

I hope the traffic's really heavy, she thought. I hope they all cook in their little tin boxes.

'Not many guests tonight, Imogen,' said Barry.

He didn't share Imogen's pleasure. Empty rooms cost him money. He handed her two plates.

'Two ham salads for table two.'

And a good afternoon to you too, Mr Hewlett!

Imogen served the middle-aged couple in the corner. Unprompted, they told her that they were going to a vintage car rally the other side of Kiddington. Imogen was halfway back to the kitchen when she heard the woman say, 'What a nice young girl!'

Funny how *nice* sounded so good whereas *beautiful*, out of the mouths of The Boys, sounded positively sinister. Imogen glanced round and flashed the couple a smile.

She was clearing the couple's dessert dishes when she saw Anthony hovering ghostlike in the archway.

'Hi,' she said.

But he darted away. She heard his tread on the stairs and frowned.

Think you can put everything right with a smile, do you?

Rewind.

Two months ago.

A girl at school. Tara. She started passing me notes in class. I couldn't believe my luck! They seemed so sincere. I was wary to start with but the notes just kept on coming. She wasn't gorgeous, just moderately good-looking. Nothing like you, Imogen. That's what made me believe. She seemed within reach, attainable, even to me. In the end, I passed one back to her with my own message on it. I signed it: Love and Affection.

God, how stupid could I get? She started showing it round her friends straight away. The Year 9 girls had a field day. They blew the message up to A3 size and posted it round school. Everywhere I went they were laughing at me, and Tara laughed loudest of them all.

I swore after that experience never to hope again. Then you came along, Imogen, and I just couldn't help myself.

I hoped.

46

I still do.

At seven o'clock Imogen made for the door. Then, turning, she looked into the shadows of the stairwell and jumped. She didn't expect to find Anthony, but there he was on the first-floor landing, half lost in shadow. He was at the window, training a camera on something in the car park. He was using a long lens.

'Anthony!'

He started back from the window and spun round.

'Sorry, did I scare you?'

She leaned forward, peering through the window. She was aware of him smelling her perfume.

'What were you taking pictures of?' The idea that he might be waiting to take pictures of her never crossed her mind.

She didn't pursue the matter.

'Can I take a look?'

He handed over the camera.

'It looks expensive.'

'The camera was a present,' he lied, 'from my father.'

No, the black eye was the present. The camera was an oversight.

'Mum bought me the lens for Christmas.'

Imogen looked through the viewfinder and twisted the grip on the lens.

'I didn't realise how close it brought things,' she said. She handed the camera back. 'Good for spying,' she said.

Anthony didn't smile.

'Have I done something to upset you?' she asked, straight out.

'No.'

'Only you seem to be avoiding me.'

He shook his head.

'So we're friends?'

47

'Yes,' he said, his voice flat. 'If you like.'

She got to the top of the stairs, not quite sure what to make of his reply, when he spoke again.

'I saw you last night, in the village.'

'When was that?'

'Dunno. Seven o'clock – maybe just after.'

He hastened to explain his presence.

'Strong sunlight hurts my eyes,' he said. 'It's the glare, you see. I prefer to go out in the evening. I walk a lot then.'

Imogen nodded, wondering what to say in reply.

'You were meeting your boyfriend.'

'Boyfriend?' Her brow crimped, then cleared.

'No, that was Kes. He took me to a meeting. His girl-friend fixed up the lift for me.'

She looked at Anthony's white, impassive face.

'So we're cool?'

There was no answer so she added: 'Friends?'

He nodded, warmth entering his voice for the first time.

'Yes, friends.'

At the bottom of the stairs, Imogen ran into Mrs Hewlett.

'Still here, Imogen? I thought you'd already gone home.'

'No, I got talking to Anthony.'

'He talked to you?' Mrs Hewlett sounded surprised.

'Yes,' Imogen told her, 'About his camera.'

'He even showed you his camera? My, you are privil-eged!'

'I don't understand.'

'Anthony's a very private boy,' Mrs Hewlett explained. 'He doesn't mix easily.'

Imogen wondered why Mrs Hewlett was telling her this. She seemed to have something she wanted to get off her chest.

'Photography is his way of communicating with people.

Sometimes I think it's his only way. I'm glad to see you two getting along so well.'

'Is that all Anthony takes then?' Imogen asked. 'People?'

'Pretty much.'

'I couldn't see anyone outside,' said Imogen. 'I wonder who he was taking.'

'Oh, he waits hours sometimes,' said Mrs Hewlett, 'just to get the right shot.'

'You make him sound like a sniper,' said Imogen.

'Do I?'

Imogen bit her lower lip, thinking.

'Anyway,' she said, 'I'd better be off. Mum and Dad will wonder where I've got to.'

She walked out into the whispery evening. Somewhere upstairs a shutter clicked.

Not as good as my first shot of you, but intriguing.

In the first pose you were newly come into my world. Now you've moved to its heart. Everything revolves around you.

A friend's boyfriend – that's what you said about the biker. Should I believe you? I wonder. I believed Tara, but you're not Tara, are you? There was no reason for you to lie. If he was your boyfriend, you would have said so. No, you were telling the truth, I know you were.

Hope is re-born.

'Enjoying the movie?' Katie asked.

Imogen gave a wry smile. The cinema – that was the alibi she'd given her parents.

They were sitting on the wall in front of Kiddington Castle, four girls and six boys, watching the insects floating in the floodlights. Danny had brought a few cans of Bud along. Katie had suggested trying to get into a pub. In her new leather jacket, and with just the right amount of slap,

Imogen might just have passed for eighteen, but she didn't want Mum's third degree if they got caught. Mum and Dad still treated her as if she was nine. She would never hear the end of it. No, this was better.

She hadn't left the house like this, of course – not the way Mum and Dad were. She put her make-up on in Danny's car. Thank goodness for Danny, Katie's boyfriend! He was eighteen and ran them around where they wanted to go. If not for him, they'd be forever stuck in Marsham.

'I'll pop over the Multiplex in a bit,' said Danny. 'Get you a movie guide.'

Emily, another of the gang, leaned across.

'Still spinning them a yarn, Imogen?' she asked. 'Do your folks still grill you about what you've seen?'

Imogen nodded. 'Sometimes.'

It was really embarrassing. It wasn't as though she got rotten drunk or did drugs or anything. It was just a lousy can of lager – one can, a way of meeting friends. Did they really want her rotting away in Marsham, sitting in the living room watching TV with them?

'Poor you,' said Emily. 'My parents remember what it was like to be young. They're really cool.'

Imogen wrinkled her nose. 'Yes, poor me.'

Anthony was still on the landing hours later, when Barry Hewlett climbed the stairs with room service for the old couple. Trixie, as usual, was in tow.

'What have I told you about lurking round the rooms?' Hewlett said. 'You'll upset the guests.'

'You think I'll creep them out, Barry?' Anthony asked. 'The phantom of Old Marsham Inn.'

He raised his hands above his head and wriggled his fingers. 'Whoo-oo-oo!' Trixie shrank back, a low growl forming in her throat. She was obviously afraid of the supernatural. Hewlett shook his head and knocked at room fifteen.

'Just clear off, Anthony.'

'Or what?'

Hewlett's face reddened.

'Go on,' Anthony demanded. 'Or what?'

The door opened.

'Room service,' said Hewlett.

Anxious that Anthony was going to make some kind of scene, he glanced around.

Anthony was gone.

Anthony slipped out into the fragrant night. While he had been standing on the landing, thinking about Imogen, the shadows had been padding around Old Marsham Inn, silky and velvety as a cat, until the dusk thickened into night. Now, out in the open, the stars were shining, as if chipped from the diamond face of eternity. Anthony breathed the evening air. His thoughts had been so full of Imogen that he had missed the dying of the light. He walked under the vault of the stars, happier than he could ever remember.

He was in Slaughter Lane. Through the trees he could see the mist gliding across New Pool and Hawkstone Pool, a milky tracery on the surface of the still waters. A spectral land for the ghost of Marsham. He walked as far as the railway trackbed. Back in the nineteen sixties there had been a line through here, from Birmingham to London, but it had been a victim of the Beeching closures.

Anthony only knew about the man who chopped the railways from the Internet, but he immediately added him to his growing catalogue of villains. Now Beeching ranked with DJs, his dad, football commentators, Barry, celebrity presenters, The Boys, all gangsta rappers and the inventor of the mobile phone. Anthony imagined a time before all that – a time when people sipped Earl Grey tea on a breeze-cooled verandah and looked out upon endless countryside. It was a myth, he knew that. Cruelty had always existed and probably in a more brutal form than now, but it was a myth Anthony longed for. He found modern life mean and brash. What he longed for was something outside of time. Beauty. He looked sadly at the briars and nettles swaying darkly below the bridge, a symbol of the slow withering of the countryside.

He stood there for some time before cutting through the woods to New Pool. The August heat was beginning to smother him so he worked his way down to the water's edge and sat on a log, watching the mist play on the surface of the lake. White ribbons of vapour were stealing through the woods too. Trees stood out from it like veins in a ghostly face. Far off he imagined the hushed murmur of the sea. Anthony looked at his reflection in the black waters and wondered.

'Do I dare hope?'

Leaving New Pool behind he made his way up through the bruised, blue-black darkness of the night to Battle Lane. He walked fast until a sheen of sweat stood out on his face and his heart thudded in his chest. He looked towards the sprinkle of lights that was Old Lane. He was ready to go back now. Before bedtime he would add the new shot of Imogen to his gallery.

Five

It was Monday morning. Ice-blue eyes followed Imogen all the way down Old Lane.

Flushed from the walk and quite oblivious to the predator's eyes, Imogen hung her jacket on a peg in the kitchen and slipped on her apron. She glanced at the Poleci jacket, £150 worth. Mum had given her a ten-minute lecture about wearing good stuff to work and not knowing the value of money, but Imogen had persuaded her to let her go out in it.

Imogen was tying her apron when she remembered Friday night in Kiddington. At the thought of Simon, she smiled. He'd been really keen on her. He'd been quite tasty too. Definitely worth snogging. Yes, snoggable if a bit Boys Behaving Sadly. In the end she'd flirted a bit, but that was as far as it went. She wasn't sure how, but she had a feeling she could do better.

It wasn't yet seven o'clock when she arrived at the Inn, but the heat enfolded her like shimmering wings. She found herself flicking at non-existent cobwebs, but it was only the beginnings of a heat rash. She stood at the threshold of the dining room and sank a deep breath. She didn't need telling that The Boys were back in town. She could hear them, all except Craig. It didn't take a genius to know why he was so quiet. He would be buried in his copy of *The Times*, using words as a cocoon.

'Two racks of toast for table five,' said Barry Hewlett.

He didn't so much as look up from buttering the golden rounds of bread. No good morning, no welcoming smile – just an order. All the social skills of a lobotomised arachnid! Victoria Hewlett's gaze touched Imogen's.

'Don't worry about old Grumpy Bear,' she said. 'He got out of bed the wrong side this morning.'

He hadn't. Hewlett had slept on a fierce argument with Anthony and woken out of sorts.

'Here she is, Boys,' said Wise, heavy-lidded eyes settling on Imogen.

She could feel him breathing on her skin. More cobwebs.

'Prettiest girl I've seen today,' Wise said.

Imogen slid away from his stare and looked around the dining room. Two men – business people or salesmen by the look of their suits and briefcases – sat at separate tables. The elderly couple were just leaving. They waved to Imogen and she waved back.

'*Only* girl you've seen today,' Imogen snorted.

Anthony put in an appearance while The Boys were working their way through a full English breakfast. Riley was the exception to the feast of cholesterol. For him it was dry toast, black coffee and lashings of self-pity. He didn't say: *Never Again.* It would have been too big a lie.

'Well, look who's here!' said Wise. 'If it isn't the White Rabbit!'

The words stopped Anthony dead in the archway. He was wearing a baseball cap and sunglasses – protection against the glare of the summer sun, Imogen guessed.

'Ignore them,' she whispered.

'I always do,' said Anthony.

Imogen knew that wasn't true. She'd seen his hurt and frustration. Anthony's face was anything but a blank page.

'Are you going somewhere?' she asked.

Anthony nodded. 'Kiddington. I'm getting the half-past nine bus.'

There was a shoppers' service, a thirty-seater bus that went from the High Street in the morning, winding through the sprinkle of picturesque villages on the way, and returned at four o'clock the same afternoon.

'I'll walk down with you,' Imogen said. 'I finish at nine.'

The look on Anthony's face told her that was what he was hoping for.

'Hey, Goz,' said Wise. 'Take off the shades a minute. Is it true you albinos have pink eyes?'

'Don't show your ignorance,' said Craig, without looking up from his newspaper. His scowl burned through the page.

Anthony and Imogen hurried from the room.

Imogen headed for the door fastening her jacket then, feeling the heat on her face, slipped it off again and tied the sleeves round her waist. Pity – she wanted to show it off but it wasn't worth a heat rash.

'Don't let them get to you,' she said.

'I don't,' Anthony replied. 'To be honest, I think they're much crueller to you. Don't you want to scream at them or something?'

'I can handle them,' Imogen said, hardly more convincing than Anthony.

'You shouldn't have to.'

'No,' she agreed, 'I shouldn't, but I want the job. Beggars can't be choosers.'

Beggars can't be choosers – wasn't that what Mum had told Anthony while she was still trying to save her marriage? It didn't convince then, and it didn't convince now.

They were about to leave when Mrs Hewlett appeared.

'Have you put your sun-block on, Anthony?' she asked.

'Yes.'

'The Factor 35 out of the cupboard? The good stuff?'

'Yes, Mum.'

'And you've got a bottle of it with you for later?'

A plug of irritation filled his throat. '*Yes!*'

'Sorry,' Mrs Hewlett said, belatedly realising she was embarrassing him in front of Imogen, 'but you know how you burn.'

'I'm short of skin pigment,' Anthony told her, 'not brains.'

With that, they stepped out into the heat. The high summer sun had burned the last of the mist off the pools and its glare was hard and direct. Sharply-edged cloud shadows raked the hillside out towards Crofton.

'She doesn't half go on,' said Anthony.

'Only because she cares,' said Imogen.

Anthony grunted as if he didn't want to admit his mother's love.

'So, what are you going to do in Kiddington?' Imogen asked.

Anthony patted his shoulder bag. 'I need film for my camera. After that, I'll get something to eat, call in at the library and Games Workshop, maybe have a walk round Kiddington castle, take a few photographs – you know, kill time till the four o'clock bus.'

'It's a long time on your own,' said Imogen.

'I've always been a lone wolf,' said Anthony. 'I like my own company.'

Imogen wondered if he had much choice.

'Good job,' she said.

Anthony waited a beat then glanced back at the Inn, adding, 'It's a lot better than most people's.'

At the junction with Chapel Street, Old Lane became

Mill Street. They passed Marsham Primary School then turned right into the High Street.

'I'll see you this evening then,' said Imogen.

She was passing the tennis courts when she heard Anthony's voice: 'You could always come to Kiddington with me.'

Imogen hesitated. Honestly, the moment you encourage them! How do I get out of this one?

'It's a kind offer,' she said, 'but I mightn't get back in time for work.'

She immediately knew how lame that would sound. There was plenty of time. To protect his feelings, she added, 'Maybe some other time.'

I'll keep you to that. Our trip to Kiddington! It's a date, then. I just wish it was today. Stupid job! That's all that's stopped me spending a whole day with Imogen. I can't believe she likes me, somebody as lovely as her.

Imagine if I'd told her what I need the films for!

To take more shots of her.

Anthony climbed the hill to Kiddington castle. He glanced at it from under the peak of his baseball cap. There was a young mother with her children, a hyperactive five- or six-year-old and an unsteady toddler clinging to a buggy as he tested his sea legs. Beyond them there was a crowd of teenagers involved in horseplay around the castle walls. Instinctively, Anthony shied away from them.

Finally, discovering a secluded spot near the keep, he took out the Pentax and loaded it with film. Snapping off the lens cap, he looked for targets. With the help of the long lens, his eyesight was a match for anyone. He wasn't interested in the rolling countryside – it was people he needed. He only shot people. The young mother was interesting, but just as he focused on her the toddler sicked half his lunch down her front. Anthony swept the lens away. The gross-out factor had no place in his photos. He had his fair share of uglies in the gallery, but it was something altogether different he was really looking for.

He was still sighting prey, blurring the possible target, when he glimpsed a familiar face among the racing figures – Tara. Remembering her premeditated cruelty, he fixed on her, twisting the focus grip until her image was sharp. Sharp and *mean*. He got off a couple of shots, then moved on. His breath caught – Jamie Smith. Anthony moved the lens around, searching. If Smith was here then Paul Jones wasn't going to be far.

There.

Anthony brought Jones into focus. The nose was mended, but more hooked, more hawk-like than previously, courtesy of Anthony's elbow.

I should go, Anthony told himself, but self-preservation didn't come into it. He was fascinated. Here were three of his tormentors, all together. He shot all three of them, one or two of their friends as well, but he didn't go. They had got his attention.

Paul and Tara started wrestling around on the grass. Finally, Paul pinned Tara's shoulders and held her down. She was giggling, cheeks blowing, hair framing her face, chest rising and falling as she put up token resistance.

It was a good picture but it came at a price. The sun must have caught Anthony's lens because the next thing to come into focus was Jamie Smith's pointing finger. Suspicion twisted his face into a tight knot. Anthony heard the angry shout: 'Somebody's spying on us!'

Anthony's heart was numb with fear. Then fear melted into horror.

'It's Albie. Get him!'

Anthony rammed the camera into his shoulder bag and took off. Tripping and stumbling, he raced down the hill.

The bag was weighing him down but he wasn't going to ditch it. It was his eye on the world.

'Albie!' came the shouts behind him. Then 'Sno-wy!'

Anthony wasn't going to stop. He remembered the scarlet burst of blood from Jones's nose. A week's suspension wouldn't be enough payback for him – he would want revenge in kind.

An eye for an eye.

Blood for blood.

How could this happen?

Is it a curse, is that it? What am I, everybody's victim? Gozzie, Snowy, Albie No. My skin, it's a white flag to them. That's it, that's what they see in me – a symbol of surrender. But I won't give up. Not this time. I won't let them hurt me. They'll never humiliate me again.

Especially not in front of Tara. She's drawn enough blood already.

I won't give them the pleasure.

Anthony spun into a back alley. His heart was banging. He felt the sweat on his palms. His mind was racing to find a way out.

He heard the pack again: 'Sno-wy!'

But how do I get away? Which way?

He remembered the camera. If he could get somewhere high and out of sight, the long lens would give him an advantage.

Then he saw it. The high rise car park. Edging to the end of the alley, Anthony darted a glance left and right then ran for the graffiti-marked stairwell of the car park. He pounded up the stairs to the third level and pulled out the camera. Panting, he trained the lens on the castle, then on the pavement below.

No sign of them, thank God!

Pulling off his sunglasses with trembling fingers, he used the back of his hand to brush the sweat from his eyes. He swept the streets again with the lens. He was about to declare himself out of danger when a face tilted in the viewfinder.

Tara.

'He's there!' she screamed.

Then the baying cry from Smith and Jones: 'Sno-wy!'

Tara's eyes lit up with contempt for him. When she put someone down, they were supposed to stay down. Anthony searched for an escape route. He saw the walkway to the new shopping mall, and ran.

Think. Think!

That's what makes you different from them. This little pig's got a cerebral cortex, a porky superbrain. Now use it. You can't outrun them. There are three of them after you. They're big bad wolves. When their blood is up like that, civilisation falls away from them. All that's left is hate.

You can't let them get hold of you.

So think.

That's when Anthony began to think.

Making an effort to bring his breathing under control, he walked into the largest of the new clothes stores and selected a shirt and a pair of trousers.

Stay calm. Don't draw attention to yourself.

Not pausing to check the sizes, he walked up to a male assistant.

'Excuse me, where are your changing rooms?'

The assistant pointed them out. Checking the front door and windows for pursuers, Anthony slipped into a changing room. Once inside, he slid down the partition wall on to the swivel seat and waited, his bag and the clothes hugged to his stomach. After a few minutes there was a knock on the door. His stomach rolled like a ship in a storm.

'Who is it?'

He heard the assistant's voice: 'They've gone.'

'Sorry?'

'The kids that were chasing you. They went down the escalator.'

Anthony looked out. From behind the sunglasses, his eyes flashed gratitude.

'How did you know they were after me?'

'Work here long enough,' the assistant said, 'and you get to see them all: the psychos, the drunks . . . the bullies.'

Anthony handed over the clothes.

'They weren't even my size,' he said.

The assistant winked.

'I know.'

Anthony got off the bus at ten to five. It took fifty minutes from Kiddington, picking up several times on the way. It dropped him on the High Street and he started in the direction of home.

When he turned into Mill Street, his heart leapt. Imogen was about fifty yards ahead of him, walking briskly, her pony-tail bobbing. She must be on her way to work. He thought for a moment of shouting to her, then dismissed the idea. It would mean passing up a good shot. He pulled out the Pentax.

'That's it, Imogen,' he said. 'Just keep on walking.'

That was when an idea occurred to him. She'd told him that if she went to Kiddington with him she wouldn't get back for work. He frowned. Maybe she meant she'd be too rushed.

Yes, that was it.

Anthony raised the camera and shot her from behind.

MARSHAM OBSERVER
Thursday, August 1

LOCAL MP CONDEMNS DETENTION CENTRE PROPOSAL

Sir Richard Gill, MP for Kiddington and Marsham, has condemned the proposal to build a detention centre for asylum seekers on land between the villages of Marsham and Crofton.

Speaking at a meeting at Kiddington Town Hall, Sir Richard said: 'The plan to dump hundreds of bogus asylum seekers on these small rural communities is a scandal. It is high time this government realised that we are living in a crowded island, struggling to come to terms with mass immigration.'

Heckled loudly throughout his speech by about a dozen protestors, Sir Richard countered: 'All that these people have

succeeded in doing is increasing my doubts about the merits of a multi-cultural society.'

Protestor Sophie Hart, from the town's Refugee Committee, said: 'Sir Richard's speech is really depressing. He fails to understand that people wouldn't cross half the world, in terrible conditions, if they weren't desperate to escape evils such as war and persecution. Speeches like Sir Richard's, which scapegoat asylum seekers, show a lack of human understanding and can only fan the flames of prejudice.'

The Refugee Committee plans to lobby Sir Richard's surgery for constituents on Wednesday night.

Six

Imogen hadn't even got her apron on when she heard Mickey Wise's braying voice. Sometimes she wondered whether this job was really worth the hassle.

'Seen this?'

She glanced into the dining room. They were on form. Five past five in the afternoon and they were in full flow. Wise was holding up the *Marsham Observer*.

'Some idiots are going to picket the local MP over these asylum seekers. Don't tell me they actually *want* all these foreigners coming over? I mean, what are they thinking? Ridiculous!'

'They want to put up a big sign at all the ports,' said Riley. 'Full up. No entry.'

Imogen exchanged glances with Mrs Hewlett.

'Barry,' said Mrs Hewlett, 'the guests on table five are getting a bit rowdy.'

Hewlett frowned. Trixie gave a little growl.

'They're only discussing the news,' he said.

'Yes,' said Mrs Hewlett. 'Loudly.'

'I tell you what,' said Hewlett, 'the moment they go over the top, I'll have a word with them.'

There was a coldness in his normally soft blue eyes. Hewlett was letting her know he wasn't about to upset The

Boys on her say-so. Imogen wondered what they would have to do to push him into action – put Anthrax in the sausages? Do a striptease on the table? Set off a thermonuclear device in the dining room?

'Take these steak and kidney pies over to table five,' Hewlett told Imogen. 'And mind you're civil.'

Imogen understood from that that her annoyance was showing. She put the men's evening meals in front of them, resisting the urge to drop them from a great height.

'That's working men's grub,' said Mickey Wise. 'You're a good girl, Im.'

'Her name is Imogen,' said Craig.

'Yes, and yours is Butt Out,' Wise snapped.

Riley spluttered out a loud guffaw. Craig looked down and started eating. Round One to Mickey Wise.

'So what do you think of all this malarkey?' Wise asked, indicating the *Observer* article. 'You're a local girl. What do you reckon to a bunch of unwashed students wanting to flood the place with immigrants?'

'You wonder what you work for,' said Riley, 'if that's what your taxes get spent on.'

'I think,' Imogen said very slowly and deliberately, aware of Hewlett's eyes on her, 'you're being very stupid.'

Wise's head snapped round. 'What did you say?'

She'd been wanting to explode her little grenade for days. It gave her quite a buzz to finally tell them how she felt.

'You're being stupid . . .' Stuff Hewlett! she thought . . . 'and racist.'

Stuff his job too if he doesn't like it!

Hewlett was already making his way to the table, in damage-limitation mode.

'I think you're the one who needs teaching manners,' Wise blustered.

He was making as if to get out of his chair when somebody beat Hewlett to the table.

64

'Leave her alone!' yelled Anthony. And in one swift move, he flung the entire contents of the gravy boat all over Mickey Wise's shirt.

I'm out of the door and flying down Old Lane, into Slaughter Lane, laughing inside, well before the gravy hits the lousy moron. Maybe I make a poor Sir Lancelot, but I've just defended my lady fair. In place of a lance, I used a gravy boat, but what the heck! It did the job. I hope it burned him, burned him good!

Honestly, getting away from Smith and Jones and teaching Mickey Stupid Wise a lesson all in one day! I'd love to see Barry's face now – Barry, in his stupid fat-guy pants, fussing over his best customers, telling them it won't happen again. Well, who's to say I don't have more tricks up my sleeve, Barry? Who's to say I haven't got a cute little box of tricks to lose all your lousy customers and reduce you to bankruptcy? Don't creep out the guests, you say?

Barry, I just did!

There was an icy glint in Mickey Wise's eyes as he looked at Imogen. When the flying gravy splashed over his shirt and up into his face, her first impulse had been to laugh. The look on Wise's face put a stop to that. When his eyes touched hers, the laughter died in her throat. She got an inkling what he was capable of.

'I'll get a cloth,' she said.

'I think you've done enough, my girl,' said Barry Hewlett. 'Get your coat.'

Imogen didn't have a coat, on account of the heat, but she knew what he meant. She was fired. She felt sick. How was she going to explain it to Mum and Dad? Oh God, they'd probably come down on the bounce. It would be so embarrassing.

'Barry,' Mrs Hewlett said, 'don't be hasty. It wasn't Imogen who threw the gravy.'

'No,' said Hewlett, 'it was your freak of a son.'

Mrs Hewlett's eyes narrowed to points of obsidian. Hewlett immediately regretted what he'd said.

'Sorry, I didn't—'

'Just don't say another word,' Mrs Hewlett hissed. 'You've said quite enough already.'

She turned to Wise.

'It wasn't hot, was it, Mr Wise?'

'Not so you'd notice,' Wise replied. 'I'm not scalded or anything.'

Mrs Hewlett smiled her obvious relief.

'If you change and give me your shirt, Mr Wise,' she said, 'I'll have it cleaned for you free of charge. We'll give you another table and the meal this evening will be courtesy of the management. I can only say that I am very sorry for Anthony's behaviour. I will have him apologize when he gets in.'

Wise fastened his stare on Imogen. 'What about her?'

Mrs Hewlett glanced at Imogen. Imogen knew what was expected of her. Much as it made her gag, she was going to have to eat humble pie.

'I'm sorry, Mr Wise,' she said. 'I spoke out of turn.'

Wise wasn't about to let her off the hook quite that easily. His eyes pinned her. He wanted more than a simple apology. Long-term grovelling was what he was after. That, and submission. Her soul laid out for him to wipe his feet on.

'Come on, Mickey,' said Craig. 'You don't want to get the girl the sack. She's said sorry.'

'Yes, lighten up there, Mick,' said Riley. 'It was quite funny really.'

He rose to his feet and wrapped a wiry forearm round Wise's neck. He gave Wise a playful hug, tousling his hair.

66

'That's the ticket, Mickey lad! Cut the girl some slack. Just think of your Lauren. I bet she's thrown the odd wobbler in her time. You're always saying how you like a woman with spirit.'

The rage dropped out of Wise's face.

'You're right,' he said. 'Give Imo a break, Barry. It's probably the heat. You know how it affects the fair sex.'

Imogen managed a reasonable imitation of a grateful smile, but inside she wanted to throw up.

The Hewletts let Imogen off early.

'Call it a cooling-off period,' said Mrs Hewlett.

Her husband grunted. He still blamed Imogen for the scene in the dining room. She'd been given a yellow card when he wanted a red.

'Do you think Anthony's all right?' Imogen asked, provoking an even louder grunt from Hewlett.

'Oh, if I know Anthony,' said Mrs Hewlett, 'he'll be roaming round the pools right now.'

Imogen stood listening. Whatever she'd thought earlier, she still wanted the job. She could hear The Boys laughing and joking in the bar with some of the locals. The detention centre was still the big topic of conversation. Neither her words nor Anthony's gravy-boat protest had taught them a thing.

'Anthony loves looking out across the water,' Mrs Hewlett said. 'It fascinates him.'

Hewlett flashed a glare that said: *I hope he falls in*.

Imogen beat a retreat but at the front of the Inn she didn't turn right towards home, but left down Slaughter Lane.

'Anthony!' she called when she came to the woods. 'Anthony, are you there?'

She looked at the coppery evening sunlight on the trees and at the sky, clear except for a few thin shreds of cloud. It was a fine, tranquil evening, from which the light was just beginning to fade, but inside Imogen was anything but calm. She took a gamble and turned towards New Pool.

'Anthony!' she called again.

She heard a twig snap behind her.

'Anthony,' she said, 'is that you?'

There was no answer, but she sensed movement in the gathering dusk. Imogen's brow creased. She was sure somebody was there.

'Hello?'

Her voice quavered just a little. Then, brushing thoughts of being followed out of her mind, she made her way down to the water's edge. It was very still, the dark columns of the trees mirrored perfectly in the surface of the pool. There was another sound, like a slithering footstep.

'Is somebody there?' she asked.

But there was no answer. Annoyed with herself for coming, Imogen started to jog back towards Slaughter Lane. Twilight was massing around her and the night sounds that were oozing out of the thickening murk told her it was time to go home. Hearing another of those sliding, slipping footsteps, she started to run faster. But before she could reach the road a dark figure stepped out in front of her.

'That son of yours will ruin my business,' Barry Hewlett snapped.

'*Our* business,' Victoria Hewlett reminded him. 'My money is tied up in this place too, you know.'

She let this sink in, then continued. 'I think there is something more important to discuss, don't you?'

Hewlett gave her a guilty look, like a dog that's eaten the Sunday roast.

'You called Anthony a freak,' his wife reminded him.

'It just came out. I was angry.'

'Not good enough, Barry,' Mrs Hewlett said. 'I've told you all the things Anthony's been through in his young life. His own father didn't want to know him. Every day he looked at Anthony as if he was unnatural. Can you imagine what that's like, Barry – to be disowned by your own dad?'

'I said I was sorry!'

'Listen to yourself!' said Mrs Hewlett. 'Barry, you're not a naughty boy, sulking because you've been told off. Anthony's the adolescent. You're a grown man, for good-ness' sake! You should know better.'

'OK, I'll watch my tongue.'

'No,' said Mrs Hewlett, 'you'll do more than that. I'll get Anthony to apologise to that pig Wise, but you'll do something for me too.'

She ignored her husband trying to get her to lower her voice.

'You'll make an effort to be the father Anthony never had.'

Hewlett turned away. His face was lost in evening shadows.

'Barry, please! Do it for me.'

He turned, the last of the light illuminating the weak, barely distinct planes of his flabby face.

'OK, I'll try.'

'Thanks,' said Mrs Hewlett.

She reached out to her husband.

'I can't resist those baby-blue eyes for long. Now come and give me a Grumpy Bear hug.'

Imogen's heart stuttered and she started to back away.

'Imogen!' said the silhouetted figure. 'Don't be afraid – it's me.'

'Anthony! Thank goodness.'

Imogen darted a glance at the woods.

'You haven't been following me, have you?'

'No,' Anthony said. 'I saw you running. I wondered if something was wrong.'

Imogen's face flooded with relief.

'No,' she said. 'No, nothing at all.'

She remembered she was supposed to be rather annoyed with him. It must have showed because Anthony said: 'Sorry about earlier. It was for the times you've stood up for me. In my own stupid way I was trying to return the favour.'

'You almost got me the sack,' Imogen told him.

The normally quiet Anthony looked incandescent.

'Barry wanted to fire you?' he roared, mad with outrage.

Imogen nodded. 'So what stopped him?'

The answer wasn't long coming.

'Mum, I bet.'

'Yes,' Imogen said. 'She was great.'

For a moment they stood silently. Night echoes swarmed in the woods. She couldn't help wondering if they were alone.

'You've got quite a temper on the quiet, haven't you?' Imogen said.

Anthony shrugged.

'What makes you so angry?' she continued. 'I mean, has something happened to you?'

Painful memories pulsed in his brain. He'd never told anyone how he felt, but Imogen made him want to talk, to get the whole filthy mess off his chest. He couldn't remember a single other person who had listened to him the way she did.

'What makes you think something's happened?' he asked. 'Is it this recessive gene of mine?'

Imogen let his words fade into the night and waited. Eventually he spoke. She had the impression of a dam breaking.

'My dad hated me,' Anthony said.

'No—'

He cut the routine protest short.

'It's true. Ask my mum. From the day I was born, he was ashamed of what he'd helped bring into the world. Great, isn't it? It's not like I've got two heads, is it? I'm missing skin pigment and my eyes flicker. Jeez! Why does it have to be such a big deal? That's why he walked out on us in the end, even though he loved Mum. He was so . . . so cruel.'

'He beat you?'

'No, no really. Once or twice, near the end, he hit me. Frustration, hatred – I don't know why he started on me with his fists.'

It was a moment before he continued.

'It wasn't physical hurt, you see – it was the things he said. That's what rips your heart wide open – the words.'

He told her about it – the way his father called him Snowman, the way Dad's eyes always stung with shame and resentment when he looked at his son, the way there was always a razor-wire barrier of mistrust between them.

Imogen's heart went out to him. It occurred to her that, thanks to her parents, she had never had to cope with prejudice and ignorance. Her parents would have been down to school at the first sign of bullying or anything like that. Only now was she beginning to see the dark shadows that surrounded other people seeping out from the cracks in her comfortable world.

'Other kids have my condition,' Anthony finished, 'and their parents love them. What's so different about me?'

'Your mother loves you,' Imogen reminded him.

She wanted to put things right, to make up for the wrong he had suffered. But all she had to offer was words.

'Yes,' said Anthony. 'She loves me, in her way.'

'What do you mean by that?'

'It took her years to stand up to my dad,' Anthony

explained. 'I always thought she loved him better than me. It made me feel like a big white nothing. I just wanted her to stand in the way when he was yelling at me, putting me down. When she did finally start taking my part, that's what made him walk out.'

He allowed his hands to flop at his sides.

'Do you mind if we don't talk about this any more?'

Imogen took his hand. In spite of the heat that still hung in the air, it felt cold – the ghost hand of a ghost boy.

'Let's walk back,' she said.

She didn't let go of his hand until they reached the Inn.

This has been the most beautiful night of my life.

Nobody has ever listened to me the way you did, Imogen – not even Mum. When you took my hand tonight I felt as though my heart was going to burst. I wanted to hold you then, to pull you to me and hold you until we were lost in the velvet darkness.

You don't know just how wonderful you are, Imogen. You can take away the pain. You can make me whole again.

'Is that you, Imogen?'

'Yes. Where are you, Dad?'

'Come through to the study,' he called.

When Imogen appeared Dad glanced up at the wall clock.

'You're late, aren't you?'

'There was a problem at work,' she told him.

'Trouble at t'mill, eh?' he said, his voice warm and welcoming. 'Tell me about it while I make you something to eat.'

'Where's Mum?' Imogen asked, following Dad into the kitchen.

'London,' Dad said. 'Have you forgotten? She's getting her article published in *New Historian* – the one about the Battle of Marsham. The editors are keen about anything to do with the English Civil War. There's a rumour the BBC are interested in doing a documentary series. Your mum could be involved as one of the talking heads. She's gone down to discuss changes to her article – you know, make it *racy*.'

He started beating the eggs.

'So what was the problem?'

Imogen told him everything, even taking off after Anthony and holding his hand. The only thing she left out was the suspicion that there had been somebody else in the woods, somebody who had followed her. She didn't want Dad getting all paranoid over it.

'You want to watch you don't give the poor lad the wrong idea,' Dad said, serving up scrambled eggs with a hint of garlic salt.

'Oh Dad!' said Imogen. 'Don't be silly. He's only fourteen, and a pretty immature fourteen at that. He needed a friend, that's all.'

'You're sure he doesn't think you're going to be more than that?'

Imogen laughed. It was a full, ringing sound, carefree as a summer breeze.

'You should have seen him, Dad. He's just a hurt little boy. I was taking care of him, like a big sister.'

Dad smiled.

'So long as you know what you're doing.'

'Don't worry, Dad,' Imogen said. 'I do.'

I feel as if I am coming out of the darkness into the light. So long a ghost, I have found someone who sees me for what I am, not for the genetic glitch nature has made me.

When Imogen looks at me, she sees through me to the

core. She looks beyond the chalkdust face, the nystagmus.
She sees my soul. She knows that I am capable of love.
And I love her.
I think she is beginning to love me back.

Seven

If Sophie Hart was looking for a recruitment officer for the Refugee Committee, she could have done a lot worse than Mickey Wise. Until the scene in the dining room, Imogen had been losing interest in the committee. She had given Sir Richard Gill's meeting at the Town Hall a miss, starting to wonder if her parents' lukewarm response to Sophie's offer didn't make sense after all.

Imogen had found her first meeting boring and one or two of the people involved in the campaign positively weird, especially the angry anarchist with one eyebrow. Now, two days later, she was once again waiting for her lift on Marsham High Street. She had only been waiting three minutes when Kes appeared on his trusty iron steed. Mum had told her how, in her experience, activists were never on time, but Kes was. Always. You could set your watch by him.

'We must stop meeting like this,' he said cheerfully.

'I know,' Imogen said. 'We'll have the villagers talking.'

There was little chance of that. The early evening streets were deserted. Even Anthony wasn't a witness to the rendezvous. Imogen tapped Kes's black-visored helmet.

'They probably think I'm going out with Darth Vader.'

Kes breathed heavily to imitate the dark side of The Force and handed Imogen the pillion helmet.

'There are quite a few of us going to Sir Richard's surgery,' he told her. 'That article in the *Observer* hasn't half raised our profile.'

'What's *quite a few*?' Imogen asked, interested.

'Oh, fifteen at least.'

Imogen pulled on the helmet and smiled to herself. The way Kes talked, if you got to sixteen you ought to be entitled to representation at the United Nations!

Imogen had to wait an hour before being ushered in to meet Sir Richard. Six other supporters of the Refugee Committee had gone in before her.

'You'll be with the Refugee Committee,' Sir Richard sighed as she seated herself. He looked at her over spectacles that were drawn down to the end of his nose.

'Yes,' Imogen said. 'How did you know?'

'Obvious, really. You're under sixty. Admission to my surgeries is usually by Zimmer frame only, I'm afraid.'

'Oh.'

Imogen hated to admit it, but she quite liked the MP. Though he stood for everything she was meant to hate, he seemed witty and pleasant.

'Still, at least you've got both eyebrows.'

'You've met Andy then,' Imogen said.

'Is he the Kiddington branch of the Committee for Anarchy International?' Sir Richard asked.

'He's a third of it,' Imogen told him.

'Three anarchists in Kiddington!' Sir Richard mused wearily. 'We must be on the verge of revolution.'

'Actually,' Imogen told him, 'there are only two in Kiddington. Andy comes from Crofton.'

Sir Richard leaned back in his chair.

'Do you want me to tell you what you're going to say?' he asked, and Imogen was aware that there was more than a hint of a sneer in his voice.

Suddenly, she didn't like him quite so much. Sir Richard went on to summarise all the arguments Imogen had rehearsed.

'Is that about right?'

Imogen nodded, confidence hissing out of her like air from a punctured tyre.

'Very well, then,' said Sir Richard, stifling a yawn, 'I'll note your concerns. Goodnight, my dear.'

Impressed that he could recall everything said to him in such detail, Imogen was stunned to silence. Without another word, she walked to the door and opened it. She saw the other members of the Refugee Committee sitting in the waiting room and felt the weight of her own humiliation. The way Sir Richard had said *my dear* ricocheted round her brain, squawking 'Failure! Failure!' Feeling her friends' eyes on her, she stopped in her tracks. She turned and gave a little cough to catch Sir Richard's attention.

'Sir Richard,' she said, while her blood was still up, 'you might think it's fun to patronise me because I'm only sixteen, but I care about this issue. I think stirring up racism to get votes is *disgusting*. The next time you say something inflammatory, maybe you should think about some innocent asylum seeker being set upon on the way home by ignorant people who believe what you say and are dumb enough to act upon it.'

Pulling the door shut behind her, she said, in her loudest voice, 'Goodnight.'

The rest of the committee burst into spontaneous applause around her.

Back at the Law Centre, Imogen found herself the centre of attention. Kes introduced three men.

'This is Hamid,' he said. 'This is Ahmed, and here . . .' He ushered a third man into their conversation. 'Here is Farid.'

'You're asylum seekers?' said Imogen.

'That's right,' said Kes. 'They're what the whole campaign is about. They fled from Afghanistan. They're waiting to hear the results of their appeal.'

'Sophie says you were really brave,' said Hamid. 'You told the MP exactly what you thought of him.'

'I wouldn't say I was brave,' Imogen answered. 'He's only a crusty old man. I wasn't brave, just angry. He started treating me like a little girl, just like . . .'

She was thinking of The Boys.

'It doesn't matter.'

Hamid and Ahmed moved away to talk to Sophie. Imogen found herself alone with Farid. There was an embarrassed silence. For a few moments Imogen was almost afraid of Farid, then she realised how ridiculous that was. Farid was eighteen but looked much younger. There were tufts of downy black hair on his top lip, masquerading as a moustache. He was tall, maybe six feet two, and impossibly thin. His legs, like stilts unable to fill his flapping trousers, reminded Imogen of a giraffe's.

'You're Farid.'

'Yes.'

'What made you come to this country?' she asked.

'My father fought for the Russians in the Eighties,' Farid said. 'He found himself on the wrong side – the losing side. After that the family had many difficult years. There were men – still are men – who have scores to settle. Eventually it got too much.'

'Where is your dad now?'

'Dead. My mother too.'

There was a finality about Farid's answer, a warning that this was a closed chapter, so Imogen didn't ask how or where his parents had perished.

'Don't you have *any* family?' she asked.

'I have an uncle. We came out of Afghanistan together.'

'And where is he now, your uncle?'

Farid shook his head, as if trying to dismiss bad thoughts.

'I don't know. We were in Europe. We lost each other.'

Imogen saw desolation in Farid's eyes. She was aware of her designer clothes and her comfortable middle-class life. She, who had never been alone, who had never felt lonely in the least, wondered what it was like to have nobody at all.

'Don't you have anybody?'

Farid looked at Hamid and Ahmed.

'I have my friends.'

He gave her a smile.

'I have the committee.'

Imogen nodded.

'I think Sophie's great, don't you?'

Her eyes touched his. She was willing him to open up, to tell her more about himself.

All he said was: 'Yes.'

Their conversation wasn't quite what she had expected. In the books she had read and the films she had seen there were lots of '. . . in my country . . .' or '. . . where I am from . . .' Epic stories flowed easily from the narrator's lips, full of passion and regret. Imogen at least expected anger about his situation. In the event Farid planted his large – impossibly large, almost fleshless hands – on his knees and waited for Imogen to speak again.

'I've got to go soon,' she said. 'My parents . . .'

She let the sentence hang in the air. Farid finished it.

'They will worry.'

'Yes,' Imogen said, becoming as monosyllabic as Farid.

Maybe sensing that she wanted rescuing, Kes appeared.

'Better get you home,' he said. 'We don't want to incur the wrath of the dreaded parents.'

'No,' said Imogen, following him to the door.

Then, turning back to Farid, she added: 'Nice to have met you. And good luck with your appeal.'

Farid sat in the corner of the room at the Law Centre, nursing an orange juice. He was joined by Andy.

'On your own?' asked Andy.

'No.' Farid indicated Hamid and Ahmed. 'I am with my friends.'

'No, I mean in this country.'

'Oh yes, quite alone.'

'You don't want to let them grind you down,' said Andy.

Farid wondered for a moment who might want to grind him down, then wondered exactly what Andy meant by grind down, then nodded sagely.

'No,' he said. 'I won't.'

'You know what you need?' Andy said.

Farid waited a beat. Andy had him stumped. He was thinking perhaps another orange juice, some nuts from one of those little bowls, or a few more minutes talking to Imogen.

'A revolution,' said Andy.

Farid smiled. 'I think we had one of those. A coup, anyway.'

'Coup?' said Andy. 'No, that's no good. Revolution, that's what you need.'

Farid stared at Andy's face.

'Why have you only got one eyebrow?'

'I fell asleep at a party,' Andy explained. 'A mate shaved it off.'

Farid pursed his lips as he processed the information.

'Was he a good friend?'

'Yes, one of the best. Anyway, I've got to find a taxi. I live out in Crofton. Total dump. All cowpats and turnip-heads.'

Andy held out a hand and Farid shook it. He didn't ask what a turnip-head was. He was afraid Andy might stay and tell him. Farid was left alone again, but he didn't feel lonely. He had the memory of Imogen.

Kes dropped Imogen outside her house on Kiddington Road.

'Thanks for the lift,' she said.

'Any time,' said Kes. 'What did you make of Farid?'

'I think he's nice. Very shy though. I was already running out of conversation when you came over. It was a bit painful really.'

Farid didn't compare too well with Simon. Si could talk for hours and hours, mostly about himself unfortunately.

'I've always wondered about his shyness,' Kes said. 'Hidden depths maybe.'

Imogen was intrigued. 'How do you mean?'

'Well, his English is great, really fluent, much better than Hamid or Ahmed, yet he hardly says a word. You can't tell what's going on in his mind.'

Suddenly Imogen was interested in Farid, more interested than when she'd actually been talking to him.

'Maybe that's the idea,' she said. 'He'll open up when he's got something to say.'

'You never know,' said Kes. 'Anyway, I'd better get back.'

She waved Kes out of sight then turned towards the house. She found herself smiling. Getting Farid to talk had been hard work, but she still wanted to see him again, to find out what really was going on in his mind. It was a change to meet a boy whose hands you didn't have to fight off. Yes, the idea of Farid was growing on her. Suddenly he was a challenge.

Unlike Katie and Emily, Imogen had never had a proper boyfriend. Mum and Dad saw to that. Great, wasn't it?

They could do all that Permissive Society stuff, but they wanted to keep her like their prim little Pollyanna.

Imogen was in bed within half an hour. She had an early start next day, serving breakfast at Old Marsham Inn. Imagine Mickey Wise's face if he knew where she'd been and who she'd been talking to! But that wasn't going to happen. Another incident like the gravy boat and she was out of a job. Soon she slept and the night shadows closed in around her. She dreamed while, out in the dark, a ghostlike figure watched her window.

KIDDINGTON CHRONICLE
Thursday, August 8

INTERROGATED: TOWN MP FACES GRILLING OVER ASYLUM SEEKERS

Sir Richard Gill, MP for Kiddington and Marsham, faced tough questioning this week from the town's Refugee Committee. The group, which campaigns for more humane treatment for asylum seekers, turned out in force at the MP's surgery this Wednesday to press their case.

Said Sir Richard: 'The campaigners put their arguments forcefully. I must say, however, that I remain opposed to the dumping of hundreds of asylum seekers on the area. It is not conducive to the health of the local community. The arrival of so many people of a different culture can only stir up tensions. The overwhelming majority of my constituents vigorously oppose the proposed detention centre and the placing of any more asylum seekers in hotel accommodation here.'

Ms Sophie Hart, for the Refugee Committee, said: 'We are asking for a complete change of policy towards asylum seekers. What they need is housing, jobs and the right to a decent life. Many refugees are skilled people such as doctors, teachers and engineers. They have a lot to contribute to the UK. Sir Richard's statements sadly do not reflect this.'

Eight

A few days later a disappointed Anthony stood in the dining room doorway. His mother was serving at table five.

'Where's Imogen?' he asked when Mum came past, balancing a stack of cereal bowls.

'Her dad's just picked her up. She gets her exam results this morning.'

She gave Anthony an encouraging smile. 'Don't worry, son, she'll be here this evening.'

This evening! That was nine whole hours away. Anthony felt a plug of loneliness in his stomach.

'What's up, Gozzie lad?' asked Peter Riley, breaking in on his thoughts. 'You look like you've lost a fiver and found a pound.'

Anthony ignored him, but he wasn't getting away that easily.

'What's your favourite pop group then, Goz?' Mickey Wise asked. 'The Bleach Boys?'

'Hey, I know,' said Riley, 'favourite Golden Oldie: *A Whiter Shade of Pale*.'

When Mrs Hewlett returned with the cooked breakfasts she saw Anthony retreating back upstairs. With a sinking heart, she glanced in the direction of table five. She knew something had been said.

*

Today was the day.

I was going to tell her how I felt. The poet Horace said it: 'Seize the day, put no trust in the morrow.' That was in 23BC. Over two thousand years later it takes me days of planning before I can even approach her. Why couldn't I have been born like Smith and Jones? I can still see Paul and Tara wrestling round in the grounds of Kiddington Castle. His kind have no problem talking to girls. They just go straight up to them and bang, they've scored. Talk about scum rising to the top!

I couldn't mention Horace around The Boys, of course. They probably think he's Homer Simpson's younger brother or something. Morons! How I would love to take Imogen out. How I would love to show her off to them, those sad, nasty, dirty old men.

In the car, coming back from Mount Carmel, Imogen's face was flushed with excitement.

'I can't believe it!' she said breathlessly. 'All As and A stars! Just how cool is that, Dad?'

Dad grinned. 'I never had any doubts,' he said. 'You're an intelligent girl.'

'What?' Imogen said. 'No doubts *ever*?'

'Well, maybe the odd sneaking suspicion you might slip down to a B somewhere.'

'Dad!' Imogen cried in mock horror. 'And I thought you believed in me, your daughter the genius.'

'Always Imogen,' said Dad, his voice dropping an octave. 'Always.'

He took the bend where Bridge Street becomes High Street and braked hard. He had the impression of a white face slanting across his vision. Somebody had stepped off the pavement in front of him. The figure pitched and seemed to roll out of sight.

'Jeez!' Dad said, unclipping his seatbelt and jumping out of the car.

'Are you all right, son?'

'Anthony!' said Imogen, recognising the pedestrian sitting holding his arm by the roadside.

Dad gave her a questioning look.

'This is Anthony Hewlett, Dad. I've told you about him. He lives at Old Marsham Inn.'

Dad examined Anthony, giving him a hand to get back to his feet, registering his pale skin, the baseball cap, the sunglasses.

'You *are* all right?' he asked again, heart still yelping giddily in his chest. 'I didn't clip you or anything?'

Anthony shook his head. With nervous fingers he straightened his sunglasses. He couldn't tell them he had been standing in the road looking in the direction of Mount Carmel School for Girls, waiting for Imogen to return. How creepy would that have been? As it turned out, he had jumped back just in time and saved himself worse injury than a scraped arm.

'You've got to be more careful, Anthony,' Imogen said. 'Cars come along these roads at ridiculous speeds.'

Dad wondered if that was directed at him.

'You look a bit shaken,' he said, 'and you've skinned your elbow. Tell you what, come back with us. Have a drink, maybe a bite to eat. Take a breather while I clean up that graze. It'll make you feel better.'

Anthony nodded and climbed into the back seat of the car.

Anthony probed the dressing on his arm with those long, fluttering fingers of his.

'You'll be fine,' said Imogen. 'No need for an amputation.'

Anthony blinked behind his sunglasses. 'I'm sorry?'

'Nothing,' said Imogen. 'I was only teasing.'

'Oh. I see.'

He didn't. The world of sarcasm, of teasing and poking fun, was a foreign place to Anthony. Rather than learn its rules he had long since closed the door on it and walked away.

'You got good results then?' Anthony said.

'Fantastic!' Imogen cried, still buzzing after seeing that row of straight As. 'I didn't dream for a minute I would do that well.'

'Why not?' Anthony said. 'Your intelligence is . . .'

Her hazel eyes stopped him in mid-sentence.

'Go on,' she said, leaning forward just a little.

Anthony looked at her raised face, the sunlight on her throat.

'. . . transparent,' he finished, his voice dying to a whisper.

'Why, Sir,' said Imogen in a mock Southern Belle accent, 'you say the darnedest things.'

He looked at her, fingers splayed across her soft, almost golden throat, as if overcome by his praise. He listened to the attempt at humour and knew he had no answer to it. For too long he had lived in a quiet world of his own choosing. Imogen's easy repartee was beyond him.

'Imogen,' said Dad, walking into the garden with a tray of soft drinks, 'you're making the lad blush.'

Say something! Anthony cried in his mind. Tell her the way you feel. Yes, the moment the father goes back inside, that's the time to do it. Say something then. Seize the day. But he didn't go back inside. Instead he pottered round the garden. Anthony swung a glance in his direction, but Imogen seemed more than happy to have him there. Why couldn't he leave them alone? Anthony could hear his own pulse booming in his temple.

'Imogen,' Anthony began.

Before he could say another word, her mobile rang.

'Katie!' Imogen cried, taking the call. 'Have you got your results? You did! Fantastic! Me? Go on, guess.'

Anthony sat holding his orange squash in both hands, sensing the beaded cold steal through him. The stupid call was taking her away from him. Frustration coiled in his stomach.

'No,' said Imogen. 'Higher! Higher!'

Her voice became a whoop of delight.

'That's right!'

She reeled off the results and squealed down the phone.

'Yes, isn't that just too wonderful?'

Dad grinned. While they had their fun, Anthony felt the old loneliness. Ever the outsider, he felt like a cat being put out for the night.

'Is that Katie?' Dad asked. 'Pity we missed her at the school. Say hello for me.'

When Mr Bayliss had invited him in, Anthony had leapt at the chance. Now, hearing her sharing her success with this unknown friend, he felt his solitude more than ever. She was his. He didn't want to share.

'I'd better go,' he mumbled.

'Do you want a lift home?' Mr Bayliss asked.

Anthony shook his head. He waved a hand under Imogen's face. She returned the wave nonchalantly. It was almost a gesture of dismissal. As he stumbled dejectedly back into the blistering heat on Kiddington Road he could still hear Imogen's laughter.

How he hated the sound!

'Simon's been asking after you,' said Katie. 'Interested?'

Imogen walked to the other end of the garden. 'Not really.'

'Why ever not? He's an absolute hunk, best catch in the Sixth Form. Emily's desperate to go out with him. He won't wait for ever.'

'Then tell Emily she's welcome,' said Imogen. 'Honestly, I'm not interested.'

'You know your problem?' Katie said. 'You're too picky by half. Or are you scared of coming out from under Mummy's skirts?'

'Katie,' Imogen said, annoyance showing in her voice, 'I'm fine.'

She finished the call and looked around.

'Where's Anthony, Dad?'

'Gone. He waved goodbye to you.'

'Did he?' A flash of realisation.

'Oh, I thought he was asking if I wanted another drink.'

She blinked in confusion.

'Didn't he say anything?'

'No, just that he had to go.'

Imogen felt a tug of anxiety. Being around Anthony was like living your life on a pane of glass. Putting down her orange squash, she walked round the house to the front gate. Overhead the sky was pure azure, uninterrupted except for a scud of light clouds. Yet the day felt anything but perfect. Imogen remembered Anthony's clinging gaze and she knew he would not have gone by choice.

'Something wrong?' Dad asked, joining her.

'I don't know. Did he seem upset when he went?'

Dad followed her gaze along Kiddington Road. 'Not particularly,' he said, 'but with that lad, how can you tell?'

Anthony would be home in five minutes. Then, thinking of Barry Hewlett's puffy face and Mum's fussing, he turned left into Chapel Street, away from the Inn. Finding himself in front of the village hall, he stepped over the low stone wall and walked round it. The front door and windows were boarded up. There were a few beer cans lying on the path, stamped flat by local teenagers who, very occasionally, used the waste ground behind the derelict building as a meeting place.

Anthony explored the outside for a while. The rusted alarm box on one wall deterred him from trying to enter. Then he saw Barry coming up the road, walking Trixie. Anthony drew back to stay out of sight. As he did so, he felt the board covering the fire exit rattle. Giving it another shove, he realised he could squeeze a hand inside and flip the emergency exit bar. A sludge of musty, cloying heat met him.

He sucked in a breath and waited for the alarm to yelp.

It didn't.

Disconnected.

It was dark inside and it took him a few moments to acclimatise to the gloom. When he did, he saw a stack of dusty plastic chairs and not much else. There were no beer cans or cigarette butts on the floor. It was obvious that nobody had been inside since it closed down. The alarm box had deterred them too.

Anthony sat with his back against one wall and pulled his legs up to his chest.

He was close to tears.

I should have known better.

You can certainly turn it on, Imogen. I was actually fool enough to think you cared. Then you go and swat me like a fly. Maybe you are like Tara. Do you get a kick out of it? Is that it? You like playing games. Build a person up, then knock them down, is that how you get your kicks? Imogen, my Imogen, I thought you were better than that.

Oh, what am I saying? You're not Tara. You're so much better than that. But how could you suddenly become so thoughtless? I heard you talking to that airhead friend of yours. Squealing over your exam results, like that, it makes me puke. I had something to say to you, the most important thing I've ever wanted to say in my whole life. Why couldn't you listen?

I've made my mind up, Imogen. You get one more chance, just one. I'll let you prove you're not like the others. I'll let you show that you see me, not the ghost boy. But if you let me down, if you turn out like them, then I'll hurt you.

I'll hurt you bad.

Part Two
ICE-BLUE EYES

One

Saturday was going to be a perfect day. Even the bruise-purple clouds that were massing in the distance could do nothing to detract from Imogen's good mood. The Boys had gone home for the weekend, taking their sad, seedy creepiness with them, and she still had the Refugee Committee's picnic to look forward to.

She was just wondering where they'd got to when the Law Centre minibus pulled into Battle Lane, with much snapping of twigs against glass. Imogen saw Farid's thin, almost haggard face pressed to one of the windows. She knew him immediately by the wispy apology for a moustache.

'Hi,' said Sophie Hart, swinging the door open and jumping down from the front passenger seat. 'Been waiting long?'

Imogen shook her head. 'Couple of minutes.'

She wasn't telling the truth, of course. She must have been hanging around for at least twenty minutes, listening for the bus's engine amid the chirping of the crickets and the sigh of the breeze. Since first thing this morning she had been thinking about the day ahead – thinking about Farid, if she was honest with herself. Then there he was, ducking down to avoid cracking his head, almost impossibly tall and rangy, like a giraffe. A giraffe with a silly, bum-fluff moustache. There was boy and man in him, vulnerability and power.

'Hello, Imogen,' he said.

She liked the way he said her name, in that sonorous, deliberate voice of his.

'Hi,' she answered. 'It's a beautiful day.'

Which was what it had just become. Farid turned his eyes towards the sky above, then looked back at her.

'Yes.'

She remembered their conversation, or lack of it, at the Law Centre. It made her wonder quite why she was so interested in Farid. He didn't do charm, that was for sure. There were no chat-up lines, no small talk. But she still wanted to talk to him, really talk to him, find out what thoughts lurked beneath the quiet man's mask. Mum had tried to explain the feeling once when Imogen asked what drew her to Dad in the first place. Hard to say, Mum had answered. You don't go looking for love. It comes looking for you. That was it exactly. It explained how she was feeling. Something had happened to her, something over which she had no control.

Then Imogen stopped. Love? Was that what she was feeling? Oh, come off it! she told herself. Talk about jumping the gun! You don't even know him. I mean, love, where did that come from? She was almost shocked at the idea.

Katie always said love was what lads promised you when they wanted something else. Imogen thought that sounded cynical, but she didn't have much to go on. She hadn't even had a steady boyfriend – a few unsatisfactory dates and a brief relationship on holiday last summer, and now she was thinking about love. You've got to be kidding! she thought. You can't have exchanged more than a dozen sentences with Farid. But that hadn't stopped her thinking about him –

thinking about him almost every minute of the day. She had always considered herself too practical, too level-headed to be swept away like this. I really am losing it, she thought.

A cool wind stirred in the branches of the trees and snapped in the baggy sleeves of Farid's shirt. All his clothes were baggy. There just wasn't enough Farid to fill them. Regretting her choice of a sleeveless top, Imogen rubbed her bare arms, wondering at the strange things she was feeling.

'You're cold,' said Farid.

She imagined him folding her in his arms, warming her with his body. Losing it? she thought. Already lost it, more like!

'No,' Imogen told him. 'Not cold, but the weather's on the turn.'

Oh great, now they were discussing the weather! She nodded in the direction of the bank of cloud on the far horizon.

'There's a storm coming.'

In confirmation, there came low grumbles of thunder, ricocheting round the hills.

'Do you think it will spoil the picnic?' Farid asked.

Imogen smiled and shook her head.

'No,' she said, 'nothing will spoil today.'

The instant she said the words she could hear the echo of his heartbeat.

Anthony was in the woods that backed on to Battle Lane. There must have been a time when part of the woods had been partitioned off by one of the local landowners because black, rotting fences sagged drunkenly among the bracken. Rusted barbed wire twisted dangerously through the undergrowth, a filament of menace running through a bright day. From under the peak of his cap Anthony watched the picnic. The dozen or so people were sitting on the grass, eating and drinking or simply talking. Anthony recognised the biker, but Kes was more interested in a red-haired girl than he was in Imogen. She'd been telling the truth – he was no rival. That gave Anthony no comfort, however, because Imogen was chatting animatedly to someone else – a tall Asian-looking man.

Anthony watched them through the lens of his camera, shooting them occasionally – and didn't he feel the limitations of photography. What he would have given for a long-distance microphone! But he didn't need to hear their words to know that there was a connection between them. Each time Imogen tilted her face to look up at the man, Anthony felt his pulse run faster. Once, her brow almost brushed the lips of the gangling newcomer.

How can you do this to me?

Aching to approach them, Anthony watched through the heavy, black-green leaves of the trees. At the sight of Imogen and Farid, fear squirmed in the pit of his stomach. There was no denying the evidence of his eyes. She liked him. She cared for him. Adrenalin surged through Anthony's bloodstream. Jealousy clogged his system like bile. He sank into the subconscious, a no-thought world of rage and envy and pain. Finally, he uttered a single word like a groan of agony.

'Imogen!'

'People-smugglers,' Farid told her, explaining how he had travelled across Europe. 'I woke in the middle of the night. There was a quarrel going on outside the lorry so I cut a small slit in the canvas with my penknife. I put my eye to the slit and there were the police. I could see so little of the world, but what there was . . .' He sighed. 'What there was, was bad. The police started beating the side of the lorry with their batons, then I heard the dogs. I knew my journey was over.'

Imogen pictured the scene, like a still from an old movie, SS guards or Cold War Russians moving along the track through the steaming night.

'And your uncle?' she asked.

'Already gone by the time I woke up. He had been protesting to the smugglers about something the night before. He had appointed himself as a spokesman for the rest of us. That's what he was like – a leader. I pleaded with him to stop, but he wouldn't listen. My uncle is a proud man. Maybe he is too proud.'

Imogen noticed Farid sometimes said *is*, other times *was*. He still had hope, but not a great deal of it.

'You think they hurt him?' Imogen asked, then, lowering her voice, 'Killed him?'

'I don't know,' Farid replied. He looked like a man who didn't want to look the worst possibility in the face. 'But I haven't heard from him since.'

'I wonder how you go on,' Imogen said. 'I mean, my life is so easy. It's predictable, good. I know exactly what I've got to look forward to: Sixth Form, A-levels, university. Sometimes I feel as though my whole future is mapped out for me. How do you get through the day knowing they want to send you back to . . .'

She held out her palms, turned upwards, in a gesture of bewilderment.

Farid took her hands, as if laying hold of her confusion and stroking it away.

'I go on because I have to. I live each day as it comes.'

To her own amazement, Imogen didn't feel one bit self-conscious about Farid's hands holding hers.

'I have no choice,' he said.

'But doesn't it drive you mad?' she asked, angry at some undefined 'they' that could do this to lost, stateless people.

'You're right,' said Farid. 'Being without a home, it makes people mad. Quite literally mad.'

He twisted a long, fleshless finger against his temple.

'I've seen them, the way they look around with hollow eyes. Despair isn't just a way of thinking – it can be an illness. It rubs away inside you until you start to die from the inside out.'

Kes was right, Farid's English was excellent. But in the August stillness he had no need of words.

'Sometimes you feel you have fallen right off the end of the earth. You have nothing – no country, no home, no family. There is no one.'

Then Imogen let three fateful words leave her lips. At the sound of her own words, she felt a ripple of goosebumps down her spine.

'There is someone.'

No!

Please, no.

You made me a promise, Imogen, with every look you gave me. Remember how you held my hand? Didn't that mean a thing? And the way you stood up for me, what was that about?

What I took for love is nothing to you. You let him hold your hands the way you let me.

Somebody should teach you a lesson.

Imogen pulled Farid back into the trees.

'Not that way,' she said.

Farid questioned her with his eyes.

'See that man?'

Farid watched a short, plump man walking his dog.

'That's Mr Hewlett, my boss.'

Hewlett bent forward, puffing out his cheeks with the effort.

'What's he doing?' Farid asked, staring at the small plastic trowel Hewlett was holding.

'He's using a poop scoop,' Imogen explained.

Farid frowned.

'To pick up the dog's business.'

'Ah,' he said. 'Very *responsible* of him.'

They looked at each other then laughed out loud. Hewlett looked around and they retreated into the woods, still giggling. They walked as far as the old boathouse on the far side of the lake. They sat in its shade.

'What was it like coming to a foreign country?' Imogen asked. 'A place with poop scoops.'

'There were plenty of surprises,' Farid said. 'They gave us straw to eat.'

'Straw?' said Imogen.

'Yes, straw biscuits. I was halfway through when they told me you had to add milk and sugar.'

'You mean Shredded Wheat,' Imogen said.

'Yes, but I didn't know that at the time.'

'And you still ate it?'

Farid nodded.

'Every crumb. I didn't want to abuse their hospitality.'

Imogen wrinkled her nose. 'Maybe a bale of straw would have tasted better,' she said.

Farid smiled. 'Definitely. It was like swallowing barbed wire.'

Suddenly Imogen had a picture in her mind of Farid as a giraffe, splaying his legs and ripping off mouthfuls from a bale of straw. She started to laugh.

'What's so funny?' Farid asked.

'You.'

'Why am I funny?'

Imogen put her hand to her mouth, but the laughter snorted out anyway.

'You're a giraffe.'

Farid's look of confusion only made her laugh louder.

'You're a strange girl,' he said.

Imogen's shoulders were shaking.

'You've got that right,' she said.

Shoot them.

Shoot him.

Shoot her.

I read somewhere that the Sioux Indians used to hate having their photographs taken. They thought the camera stole their soul. That's what I want to do to you, Imogen – steal your soul the way you stole my heart. You've betrayed me but I'll find a way to pay you back, don't you worry. I'll make you wish you'd never played with me this way.

You're happy now but believe me, when you lose your soul you'll be sorry.

'So I'm a giraffe, am I?' Farid asked.

Imogen nodded, her giggles subsiding. He had looked at her a little too long and a little too hard, and she blushed. Her shoulders were against the wall of the boathouse and Farid was very close. She found herself biting her lower lip.

'I like the way you do that,' Farid said.

Imogen was aware of the sky turning into a cataract of tumbling purples, indigos and violets around them. Fat, cold drops of rain had already started falling in the bracken.

'We'd better get back to the others,' she said. 'They'll wonder where we've got to.'

While the farthest third of the sky was as puffy and bruised as a boxer's face, directly overhead the sun still shone and the dark, sharply-defined shadows of high summer closed around them.

'I would like to see you again tomorrow,' Farid said. 'When there are no others to go back to.'

Imogen nodded and they made arrangements. When they had finished, she felt slightly guilty, as if they had done something wrong. But that was stupid.

'You asked me something earlier,' she breathed, looking away from him. 'How the names of the lanes came about.'

It was obvious Farid was no longer interested. They were going to meet again next day. A line had been crossed. Now he only had eyes for her.

'The lanes,' Imogen struggled on. 'Battle Lane and Slaughter Lane. There was a skirmish here in the English Civil War.'

She waved her arm.

'They say these woods rang with the clash of swords. England wasn't the way it is now. It was father against son, brother against brother.'

'Like Afghanistan.'

Imogen shrugged. 'Maybe. My mum knows all about it.'

Her face tilted towards Farid's.

'There was bloodshed here. Men probably died right where we're standing.'

Farid didn't say a word. He just looked at the sunlight on her face.

'You think this is a place of death,' he said.

'Silly, aren't I?' Imogen said.

'No,' Farid said. 'There are always two worlds. In the world above things go on as normal. People meet, talk, fall in love.'

'And in the world below? What happens there?'

'There is darkness, the worst men can do to each other. No matter how comfortable you think you are, the darkness is always waiting to break through.'

'So you don't think I'm silly?'

'No, I don't think you're silly at all.'

TWO

It was halfway through clearing the breakfast dishes next morning that Imogen remembered:

Sunday! You idiot, Imogen! There's no bus on Sundays.

What was she going to do? She had arranged to meet Farid off the Kiddington bus at half-past nine. They were going to spend the whole day together – at least that was the idea. But there was no bus, no service at all. Not on a Sunday. In her eagerness to see him again she had actually forgotten what day it was.

Forgotten what day it is? Oh, who's going to swallow that? Farid's bound to think I'm messing him about.

Her heartbeat quickened. He would feel so let down. There had to be something she could do.

Of course! I'll phone him.

She had the card for his B&B. She glanced round the dining room. The handful of guests had gone. In ten minutes she would have finished her early shift. She caught Barry Hewlett's eye.

'Do you mind if I make a call?' she asked.

'Suit yourself,' said Hewlett. 'It's not as if we're run off our feet.'

He gave the dining room a doleful stare. Breakfast had only been served at two tables that morning.

'Thanks.'

Hurrying to the furthest corner of the room, Imogen called Directory Enquiries. Armed with the number of the Carnforth House Hotel, she tapped in the number. At least she could explain her mistake to him.

She asked for Farid's room. There was an audible buzz of hostility in the receptionist's voice. Imogen chose to ignore it. Finally there came a strongly-accented voice. Her heart leapt.

'Farid?' she asked.

'No, this is Ahmed.'

'You share a room?'

Farid hadn't even told her that. Too proud, she thought.

'Yes, who is this?'

'Oh, sorry,' she said. 'Imogen, from the Refugee Committee. Is Farid there?'

'No,' said Ahmed. 'I haven't seen him. He must have gone out before I woke up this morning.'

Imogen sighed, then dictated a message for Ahmed to give him when he returned. Disappointed, she hung up.

'Bad news?' Hewlett asked when he saw her face.

'I missed a friend,' Imogen told him.

Hewlett nodded, as if he knew exactly what she was talking about.

'You might as well get off home,' he said. 'I can manage here. At least there'll be something for you to do tonight. The Boys will be back in town.'

Imogen faked a smile and headed for the door.

A friend!

Is that what you call him? You looked more than friends yesterday afternoon at the boathouse.

That's right, I was eavesdropping on your conversation from the hallway, just like I was watching your little tête-à-tête yesterday. They don't call me the ghost for nothing. I

*can drift unseen into any nook and cranny. When you don't
have a life of your own, you get good at spying on other
people's.*

*Have a date, did you? So what's happened? Has he stood
you up? Well, boo-hoo! I feel so sorry for you. Maybe you
should stick to your own kind. Couldn't you see, Imogen?
You had somebody who loved you. That's right, here on
your doorstep. But you had to go for something different,
didn't you? Well, I hope he's dumped you. Then you'll
know exactly how I feel.*

Imogen stepped out into bright sunlight. It had rained
overnight but now the heat of the morning sun was burning the damp off the roads. Old Lane was steaming. Not
that she paid any attention. Her mind was full of Farid.
Would he think she'd done it on purpose? Would Ahmed
remember to pass on her message?

As she plodded along the lane, Imogen felt a pinch of
misery. A whole day without him! How could something
so new have become so necessary? What was she going to
do with herself? The day had started so brightly. She had
virtually flown to work, listening to the staccato beat of
raindrops on her umbrella. Just hours ago, she hadn't had a
care in the world. But now . . . Reaching Mill Street, she
cursed.

The umbrella!

Could anything else go wrong? She'd left it at the Inn.
With her luck it would pour down this afternoon and she
would arrive at work like a drowned rat.

'Stupid day,' she said out loud. 'Stupid *me*.'

With that, she turned right onto the High Street, and
gasped. There, standing by the bowling green, tall, straight
and impossibly thin, was Farid.

'You're here!'

She ran to him and threw her arms round his neck. She

wondered what he would think of her, throwing herself at him like that. Confused, she took a step back and started fiddling with her hair. She needn't have worried. Farid grinned, like a little kid who'd been allowed out on his own for the first time.

'How did you get here?' she asked. 'There's no bus service today.'

'I know,' said Farid. 'I realised your mistake when I checked the timetables.'

'Why did you do that?'

'Ever since I came to this country, I plan everything very carefully.'

He took a step towards her.

'That isn't all. I didn't want anything to go wrong today. I wanted to be absolutely certain of the time.'

He looked at her and she felt her heart stop.

'I couldn't imagine the day without you.'

They embraced and their first kiss fizzed through Imogen. Then she pulled away.

'Just a minute,' she said. 'If there was no bus, how did you get here?'

Farid stroked a lock of her blonde hair behind her ear.

'I walked.'

'From Kiddington!' she cried. 'How long did that take?'

'Just over two hours. You must remember, Imogen, when you have crossed half the world, a few miles is nothing.'

Why did I ever believe in you?

You led me on, Imogen. You made me think you cared. Now look how quickly you've transferred your affections – and to him, somebody without a home, without money, without a future! Well, congratulations! Some catch, Imogen. I hope you're both very happy.

*

'Where are we going?' Farid asked as Imogen led the way into Mill Street.

'The Water Gardens,' said Imogen.

She patted her shoulder bag.

'I packed a picnic for us.'

She lowered her eyes, wondering what Farid would make of the day out she had planned.

'There isn't that much to do in Marsham,' she explained. 'The Water Gardens is about it.'

'It sounds wonderful,' said Farid.

Wonderful! That's what he said. Imogen could hardly believe the change in him. So quiet, so monosyllabic at first, now Farid was positively gushing.

'Where are they, these Water Gardens of yours?'

The pair were standing at the corner of Mill Street and Chapel Street.

'That way,' she said, pointing. 'Down Marsham Lane. It's about ten minutes' walk.'

She was about to show the way when she spotted a familiar figure across the road. Farid saw her forehead crease.

'What's wrong?'

'Nothing,' she told him. 'Just this odd boy I know. Do you mind if I go over and see him? It will only take a minute.'

Imogen had noticed Anthony immediately. He had jumped back the moment she looked his way, but it was him all right. He had turned and was running in the direction of the old village hall. The feeling had been growing for some time that he was spying on her. Now she was certain. He'd been watching them through that stupid camera of his. She felt like smashing the thing.

'I didn't see anyone,' said Farid.

'I did,' said Imogen. 'Come with me.'

They walked past the village hall and stopped.

'Did you see where he went?'

Farid shook his head. They retraced their steps.

'I wonder if he found a way in here.'

Imogen peered through the dusty windows.

'Anthony?' she called.

There was no answer. Judging by the expression on Farid's face, he thought she was imagining things.

'Anthony?'

Imogen tried the front door then walked round the back.

'Farid,' she said, 'give this panel a tug, will you?'

Farid looked around.

'Isn't this illegal?' he said uncertainly. 'It could get me in trouble.'

'Please,' said Imogen.

Reluctantly, Farid pulled back the panel. Slipping inside, Imogen pushed the fire door. It swung open.

'I knew it!' she said.

She reached out and touched Farid's arm.

'You stay here,' she told him. 'You don't need to get involved.'

Farid nodded and walked round to keep watch through one of the grimy windows. He saw Imogen cross the floor to confront somebody.

A ghost boy.

'Anthony,' said Imogen, 'would you like to tell me what you're doing?'

Anthony was sitting in the far corner of the hall, elbows on his knees, head sagging between his shoulders. Curled up like that, he reminded Imogen of a bespectacled Gollum. Anthony said nothing. Imogen tried again.

'You've been spying on me, haven't you?'

Still Anthony didn't say a word.

'Look,' Imogen said, the flash of temper she had felt starting to drain away, 'I'm not angry with you. It's just –

Anthony, you've got better things to do with your life than follow me around.'

She knelt down and tried to look into his eyes. Instinctively, she reached for his hands. He withdrew them.

'Anthony, have I done something to upset you? If I have . . .'

At last Anthony spoke.

'I want you to go.'

'If we could just talk,' Imogen said.

'Go,' he said. 'Now.'

Imogen stood up. This alone was an admission of defeat.

'If that's what you want.' She waited a beat. 'Is it?'

Anthony gave the briefest of nods.

'See you then,' Imogen said.

Anthony didn't answer.

'Who was that?' Farid asked as they turned into Marsham Lane.

'Anthony,' Imogen replied. 'He lives at Old Marsham Inn. That's where I work.' She sighed.

'He's a pathetic creature,' she said. 'Dad tried to warn me about him, but I wouldn't listen. He was right. Anthony's got a crush on me, you see.'

'Crush?'

'He likes me.'

Farid smiled.

'Who wouldn't?'

Imogen shook her head.

'You don't understand,' she said. 'It isn't always a good thing. People sometimes get feelings for you. You feel their eyes all over you. It can be quite flattering . . . or it can be horrible.'

Farid listened but he only heard the rhythms of his own life. After the pain of loss, after spending so many weeks as a reviled stranger, the promise of happiness drowned out everything else.

'It's a long time since anyone had feelings for me,' he said, taking her hand. 'This could never be horrible.'

Imogen leaned her head against him and put aside her troubled thoughts.

'Of course not,' she said.

Three

It was a long time before Anthony moved. He sat in the empty village hall, looking inside himself, staring bleakly through a mental window into his soul. Being near Imogen all that time had been hard. He had felt her breath on his face, the electric charge of her fingers on his hand, and he had had to face one simple fact. She couldn't be dismissed as easily as a nobody who took pleasure in hurting him. Whatever she had done to him, and why ever she had done it, it hadn't been to be wilfully cruel. If anything, that made it even worse. She had rules of her own, ways so far beyond his understanding that it hurt him to try to make sense of them. So he sat in the gloom and the dust and the heat, and he wondered. His mind toiled through the mysteries of the girl, and then became shipwrecked on them. How she could be so understanding one moment, how she could hold his hand, touch him and then, without a word of explanation, forget him and give herself to her stranger?

Anthony felt crushed by the encounter, bewildered by her confusing niceness. Enemies – Dad, Tara, Barry, Smith and Jones – he could handle. What were they but one-dimensional human beings with rejection and pain written all over them? But what about Mum, Imogen, these many-dimensional puzzles of people, his confusing and inconstant friends – what was he to make of them? Whatever their intentions, they got under his skin more effectively, cut him more deeply.

Imogen and Farid had to weave their way between the hundreds of vehicles that packed the Water Gardens car park. Marsham Water Gardens attracted visitors from fifty miles around. Some came for the large Garden Centre. Others were drawn to the many species of tropical fish, reptiles and amphibians that were on display in the light-dappled walkways. Still others enjoyed the stroll through the tranquil paths with their many fountains. Usually, Imogen would have dismissed the place as Wrinkly Alley. Now it was simply somewhere for her and Farid to be together. She paid for their tickets and led the way past a large concrete pool stocked with Koi carp.

'Beautiful, aren't they?' Imogen said.

Farid didn't answer. He was still thinking about the ghost boy. When he did speak, it was to discuss Anthony.

'Does the boy disturb you?' he asked.

'Anthony? No, of course not.'

But her voice said otherwise. She had answered quickly, her voice becoming higher than usual.

'He's a sad boy,' she said after some moments. 'His father disowned him.'

Farid interrupted. Imogen detected an edge of steel in his voice.

'But he is not alone.'

At that moment he wanted all of her. She could have no other friendships. She was the future he had promised himself, she was the England of which he wanted to be part. She was safety, warmth, life.

'No,' Imogen said, thinking of Mrs Hewlett. 'He's not alone. He has a mother who dotes on him. All the same . . .'

'Dotes? What is that?'

'He is very alone, lost.'

Farid didn't like the way her voice softened.

'So you have feelings for him?'

Imogen looked hurt. 'He's a friend.'

Her voice crumpled. 'At least I wanted him to be.'

Her hand touched Farid's. 'You've no need to be jealous.'

Farid nodded. After a moment's uncertainty a smile flooded his face. He believed her totally.

'You seem attracted to us,' he said with a smile, 'your lost boys.'

Imogen returned the smile.

'The animals are this way,' she said.

Anthony walked. It felt as if someone had opened an oven door. All around him the shimmering heat created an invisible strait-jacket of dry-toasted air that seemed to squeeze the life out of you, reducing you to a husk. He walked with a strange, plodding step as if drunk, but what afflicted him was more disorienting than alcohol.

'I don't understand,' he murmured. 'You were so . . . lovely.'

Then a voice broke in on his thoughts. A Renault Megane was pulling into the Inn car park.

'Hey Goz, old mate!' shouted Mickey Wise. 'Talking to yourself now? First sign of madness, that is.'

Anthony looked through Wise as if at some point in another, different world where he and his kind didn't exist, and made his way to the back door of the Inn.

'What's the matter?' Wise called after him. 'Cat got your tongue?'

Anthony walked on. He didn't turn round or react in any way.

But he heard.

*

Imogen and Farid were sitting by the fountains when Imogen's mobile rang.

'Oh hi, Mum,' she said. 'No, we're OK. We've got a packed lunch.'

Farid heard the buzz of Mrs Bayliss's voice over the phone.

'Tea?' said Imogen. 'No, she'll be gone by then.'

Farid raised an eyebrow. Imogen gave him a guilty glance.

'I'll get something to eat at the Inn,' Imogen said, bringing the call to a close. 'That's right. I'll go straight from here to work. Yes, I'm halfway there already.'

'She?' said Farid as Imogen slipped the mobile into her bag.

He sounded more amused than annoyed.

'Sorry,' said Imogen. 'Just a little white lie. Mum and Dad think I'm out with Katie, a girlfriend. It's not that I'm embarrassed about you. It's not to do with you being a refugee or anything – Mum and Dad aren't like that. It's just . . .'

Farid ended her sentence.

'They want to protect you. That's it, isn't it?'

Imogen nodded.

'You probably think I'm just a spoilt kid,' she said, 'but I don't want to upset them. They're not keen on me having a boyfriend. They think I should concentrate on school. That's the trouble with being an only child – they smother you sometimes.'

She still felt as though she needed to explain herself.

'Plus you're eighteen. That wouldn't go down too well.'

She wrinkled her nose and said, teasingly, 'You're an older man.'

Farid held up the flat of his palm.

'You have no need to explain,' he said. 'I am from Afghanistan, remember.'

His words brought thoughts of *burkhas* and women sitting in the shadow of their men. Imogen knew there had been a time when some Afghan women had worn Western dress, but it must be strange for Farid seeing the teenage girls walking round the Gardens in their shorts and crop tops.

'You're not offended, then?' she asked. 'That I want to keep you secret for now.'

'I don't believe you could ever offend me,' Farid said.

Imogen moved closer to him, unaware of the stares of some of the Water Gardens' visitors.

A mile away in his room, Anthony sat a long while staring at his gallery. Imogen was still the sun and everyone else the planets and moons that orbited around her. Twice he rose to tear her photograph down from the gallery. Twice he sat down again, unable to destroy an image that had become so precious to him.

'My Imogen,' he said.

The way he said it, it could have been *My life*.

As he sat staring at the photos on the wall the days ahead seemed to form a long tunnel, a lonely path leading nowhere.

It was mid-afternoon before Imogen and Farid left the Water Gardens.

'What time are you going home?' Imogen asked.

'Why?' Farid asked, the ghost of a smile playing on his lips. 'Do you want to get rid of me?'

'No,' Imogen said, 'of course not, but if you're going to walk back . . .'

'Don't worry about me,' said Farid. 'I have crossed a continent. I think I can manage Marsham to Kiddington.'

Imogen laughed. 'I'm sure you can.'

'I could wait until you finish work,' Farid said.

'What will you do all that time?'

'Walk in the woods. Throw stones at the lake. Don't worry, I will find something to do.'

'Are you sure?' Imogen asked. 'You won't be bored?'

'I will be seeing you again afterwards,' Farid said. 'Why would I be bored?'

They walked the rest of the way down Old Lane to the Inn without speaking. Words didn't seem necessary.

Mrs Hewlett checked on Anthony just before she had to start the evening meal.

'Anthony?' she called.

When there was no answer she rapped on his door.

'Anthony, are you there?'

She pushed the door open and glanced inside his room. What she saw made her frown. On the carpet lay a photograph cut into tiny pieces. Kneeling down to look at them, Mrs Hewlett started arranging the pieces. It was some moments before she was able to make sense of them. When she did her heart twisted.

It was a photograph of Imogen.

Farid walked beside New Pool. There was nobody with him but he was not alone. Imogen was with him: the memory of her smile, her scent, her laughter. In the dust of his home streets he had known fear, on the cold high-ways of Europe too where he had become, for the first time in his life, quite alone. Suddenly there was hope. Somebody saw him for what he was.

He had been walking for forty minutes when he noticed the old boathouse. The small jetty to which the anglers' rowing boats used to be moored had rotted away long ago. All that was left was a line of poles sticking out of the water. But Farid didn't see decay. Life was too beautiful for such thoughts to touch him.

Digging his hands into his pockets he wandered as far as the boathouse. There wasn't much to see – just a rickety shed, a few timbers, the odd rusting chain hanging from the ceiling. He looked around for a moment, sniffed the musty air then, with a smile, sat down with his back to the wall and settled in to wait for Imogen to finish her shift.

Imogen met Farid in the car park.

'You managed to kill the time then?' she said.

'I found a hut by the lake,' Farid said.

'The old boathouse?'

Farid nodded. 'I stayed there for a while. We could go back there.'

Imogen's eyes flashed.

'Just to sit and talk,' Farid said hurriedly. 'I think it might be better if we kept out of sight.'

'I can't stay out late,' Imogen said. 'I've told Mum I'm staying on at work. I think she believed me but I don't want to push it.'

Farid nodded.

'Tell me when you want to go home and I'll walk you back,' he said.

They took the fork of the road into Battle Lane and walked through the woods as far as New Pool. The sun hung low in the sky staining the rotting walls of the old boathouse red.

'Did many die here?' Farid asked. 'In your Civil War.'

'I don't know,' said Imogen. 'It was hundreds of years ago. Mum's the expert. I think what happened here was just a skirmish.'

Farid questioned her with his eyes.

'A small battle,' she explained.

Farid looked back at the fork with Slaughter Lane.

'It is hard to imagine this as a place of blood. It's so still, so beautiful.'

He threw a stone at the surface of the lake.

'But dark can lie beneath,' he said, watching the evening light explode around the stone's entry point. 'The world is half darkness.'

'Even here?' Imogen asked.

'Maybe,' said Farid.

He looked at the setting sun.

'Yes, even here.'

In the woods a shadowy figure was watching the couple. He especially watched Imogen: her long, blonde hair, the curve of her hips, the lithe movement of her body. Ice-blue eyes penetrated the gloom. He loved her youth, and he resented Farid, despised his familiarity, and hated the way he slipped an arm round her waist. Most of all, he hated their youth and their happiness. When they kissed temper flared in his brain and the pulse in his temple throbbed madly.

All around him, the darkness resonated with the sounds of the gathering dusk, and before long the night sounds were throbbing inside him, moving like tremors in the air. He clenched his fists until his fingernails left white crescents in the skin of his palm. There were tears in his eyes and the sunset set fire to the clouds. His heart swelled with the sound of the wind in the trees.

By the time the grainy twilight started to obscure the forms of Imogen and Farid, the watcher was screaming inside as he had screamed so many times before in his fifty years.

Where are you, Imogen?

I went looking for you, but I couldn't find you. You're with him, aren't you?

You're with him somewhere.

*

'We'd better go,' said Imogen, looking into the thickening gloom. 'They'll be worrying. They might even phone the Hewletts, then I'll really be in trouble.'

'I will walk you back,' said Farid, moving towards the door of the boathouse.

They were at the fork of Battle Lane and Slaughter Lane when Imogen's mobile phone rang.

'Oh no!' she said. 'That'll be Mum.'

But it wasn't.

'Sophie!' said Imogen, surprised. 'What's the matter? You sound upset.'

She listened for a few moments.

'Yes, he's here.'

She exchanged glances with Farid.

'Letter,' she said. 'What letter?'

She turned to Farid.

'Did you get a letter yesterday?'

Farid shook his head.

'We don't always collect our letters every day,' he said. 'I don't get that many. I've no family left so who's going to write to me? You have to ask for your mail at Reception. Yesterday I didn't go. I was at the picnic.'

Imogen conveyed the information.

'No,' she said, 'Farid hasn't looked at his mail yet.'

She listened for a while then ended the call.

'Is something wrong?' Farid asked.

'The hotel staff gave Hamid and Ahmed their post this morning,' said Imogen. 'The letters looked official.'

The words froze in her throat, and then finally she spoke.

'Farid, their appeals have been turned down.'

She swallowed hard.

'They're going to be deported.'

Farid squeezed his eyes shut. It was the news he had been dreading.

'When?'

'With immediate effect, according to the letters.'

'Is there a letter for me?' Farid asked.

Imogen nodded.

'Sophie says Hamid and Ahmed have taken refuge in the mosque. What are you going to do?'

When Farid returned her glance his eyes were empty.

The watcher sensed the emergency and moved through the bracken to get closer to Imogen and Farid. The evening stirred, tracing filigree patterns of cold on his skin. The web of a deepening dusk hung in the trees. From nowhere a night wind sprang up, whipping black rain through the threshing trees. He watched the couple hurrying towards the centre of Marsham village. When they carried on past the Inn he broke off his secret pursuit. He looked up and saw the ghost boy watching from his window. Another pair of eyes watching Imogen, wanting her.

But she will be mine.

'Is that you, Imogen?' Mum called.

'Yes, it's me.'

Mum met her in the hallway.

'You're soaked!'

'I got caught in the rain.'

Mum consulted her watch.

'And what time do you call this?'

'Sorry Mum.'

Imogen took a gamble that her parents hadn't called the Inn.

'I got talking to Anthony,' she said. 'I lost track of the time.'

'Mmm,' said Mum. 'Well, I'll tell you this, next time you're this late you'll be grounded for a week. Do you understand?'

'Yes, Mum.'

'You might think you're fireproof, but things happen. You've got to be sensible. Now, get changed out of those wet clothes. Honestly, Imogen, I thought you had more sense.'

In the bathroom Imogen changed into her dressing gown and towelled her hair. She looked at herself in the mirror. Wouldn't Katie get a shock? She was always telling Imogen to lighten up, tell her parents to get stuffed and go out and have some fun. In spite of all Katie's advice, Imogen had more or less stayed out of the dating game, the snogs, the dumpings, the breaking up and making up. Now she'd fallen head over heels in a day. What would the gang think? Propping open the bathroom window, she looked down Kiddington Road towards the village hall. Like Ahmed and Hamid, Farid had his place of sanctuary.

Four

The world isn't just light, Imogen knew that, but until now she hadn't understood just how fragile is the balance between normality and chaos. Never before had she felt so acutely the clawing fingernails of night. She hadn't felt the possibility of loss in all its keenness. She felt it now. The ground was opening and her trust in the world around her was sliding into it.

Long before Imogen had to be at work she was up, padding round the kitchen in her bare feet, darting anxious looks at the door. She quickly made Farid some sandwiches and packed them in clingfilm. She dropped a few cartons of fruit juice in her shoulder bag and finally added some chocolate bars. She heard Dad's tread on the stairs.

'Up early this morning, aren't you?' he said.

'Something woke me up,' she said. 'I couldn't get back off to sleep.'

The explanation satisfied him. Why wouldn't it? Feeling slightly guilty that she had lied, Imogen headed for the front door.

'You don't have to go out yet, do you?' Dad said, glancing at the wall clock.

'Mr Hewlett asked if I could go in early,' Imogen explained. 'There are a few more guests than there were.'

The lies were piling up, and getting easier all the time.

'So he kept you late yesterday,' Dad said. 'Now he wants you in early. This Hewlett's a bit of a slave-driver, if you ask me.'

'It's OK, Dad,' Imogen replied. 'I'm enjoying it at the Inn.'

'You're sure?' Dad asked. 'I can soon have a word if you think he's pushing you too hard.'

'No, that's all right,' said Imogen, steadying her voice. 'If it gets too much I'll soon say something.'

'So long as you're not doing too much,' said Dad.

She gave him a peck on the cheek.

'Dad, I'm just fine.'

There was a small kitchen in the village hall. It had been used to make the tea for the Women's Institute. It was there that Farid had slept or, to be more precise, lain down for the night. After the news from Kiddington there was no sleep to be had. The moment he heard the back door being pushed open he flattened himself against the wall. His mind called up images of uniformed men with dogs, of splintering doors and forced removal. Was that to be his future? His stomach clenched as somebody moved into the building. Then he heard Imogen's voice.

'It's me,' she said. 'I've brought you something to eat.'

She handed him the food.

'It isn't much, but I didn't want Mum and Dad getting suspicious.'

'It's good,' said Farid, starting to eat. '*You* are good.'

'I listened to the news on the radio,' Imogen told him. 'It said there were *three* men taking refuge in the mosque. They don't seem to know you aren't with Ahmed and Hamid. Could be Sophie and the mosque are letting them think that way. I think they're doing it for you.'

But Farid's face fell.

'I should be with them,' he said.

'And what good would that do? Your friends wouldn't thank you for giving yourself up.'

Farid stared miserably at the floor. Regardless of what Imogen said, he could feel his life disintegrating around him.

'You could be right.'

'I *know* I am,' Imogen said. 'Besides, I don't want to lose you.'

Tears welled in her eyes.

'It's all so cruel. Why does it have to be like this?'

Farid shrugged helplessly.

'I don't think I am the right person to ask.'

'Maybe not,' said Imogen.

She rummaged in her bag.

'Here,' she said. 'I brought you something to read.'

Farid glanced at the book's spine.

'*To Kill a Mockingbird*,' he said. 'What's it about?'

'Justice.'

Farid shook his head sadly, as if saying it was a rare commodity in his life.

'I saw somebody reading it recently,' Imogen explained. 'I thought of you.'

She kissed him.

'Look, I've got to go. I'll try to bring you something else on my way home. Stay out of sight.'

Farid managed a smile.

'You must do something for me,' he said. 'Talk to Sophie.'

'I will,' said Imogen. 'As soon as I can.'

At the door she looked back.

'It'll be all right.'

But neither of them truly believed that.

Mrs Hewlett couldn't put it off any longer. She had to talk

to Anthony about the photograph. Seeing it cut up on the carpet like that had disturbed her. She had lost sleep over it. Anthony was such a gentle boy usually. He was hurt and vulnerable, true, but she had never seen such anger in him before. Even that incident at school was in self-defence, a heat-of-the-moment thing. And what could he possibly have against Imogen? Wasn't he supposed to have a bit of a soft spot for her?

'Anthony? Anthony, are you in your room?'

She tapped on the door.

'Anthony?'

'What do you want?'

She could sense his defences going up already, but she was determined to have this out with him. She palmed the door open and walked in.

'Well?' Anthony asked again, without so much as looking up. 'What's up?'

'Have you quarrelled with Imogen?'

Anthony stiffened. Other than that, he didn't say anything.

'I found the photograph – at least what used to be a photograph.'

'I was a bit bored,' said Anthony. 'I just started cutting. It doesn't mean anything.'

He looked up and saw the blank disbelief in his mum's eyes.

'Bored,' he repeated.

'You're sure there's nothing else?'

Anthony shook his head.

'Anthony,' Mum said, 'you would tell me if something was wrong, wouldn't you?'

'Mum, what exactly are you thinking?'

He flicked a glance at her.

'There's no need to worry,' he said. 'It's not like I'm an apprentice psychopath or something.'

'I didn't say you were, love. I'm trying to understand,

that's all. Cutting up Imogen's photograph – it seems such an odd thing to do.'

Anthony pulled on his trainers and made for the door.

'You think?'

'Don't you?'

Anthony looked at her for a moment, then shrugged and brushed past her.

'Suit yourself.'

In the breakfast room, The Boys were on form.

'I see your refugee friends are in the news,' Wise said, jabbing a finger at his newspaper.

Imogen craned to see.

Standoff! the headline screamed.

'Think that's right, do you?' he asked, his eyes boring into her.

'I don't want to quarrel with you,' she said, immediately aware of Barry Hewlett watching from across the room.

'But you support them, don't you? You think it's OK for them to break the law?'

She wanted to argue back, but she was aware of her duty to Farid. One careless word could seal his fate.

'I think it's so sad that things have to be like this,' she said. She despised the weakness of her answer.

'Welcome to the real world, my darling,' said Wise, in a tone so patronising Imogen almost gagged on it. 'However you feel, this country can't sort out the world's problems. We've got to look after our own.'

Imogen rolled a reply round her mouth then swallowed it back.

'Will it be your usual?' she asked.

The Boys looked disappointed. Suddenly she wasn't rising to the bait.

'Yes, you bring us our breakfast, that's a good girl,' said Craig.

Imogen met his sad, sympathetic eyes. She smiled a thank you for coming to her aid and headed for the kitchen.

Imogen was clearing The Boys' table. She had just breathed a sigh of relief that they had gone to work when Mrs Hewlett came over.

'Imogen,' she said, 'can I ask you something?'

Imogen immediately thought of the confrontation in the village hall.

'Have you had words with Anthony?'

'Why do you ask?'

'No reason,' said Mrs Hewlett. 'Just an impression, that's all.'

She hastened to reassure Imogen.

'I'm not accusing you of anything, you understand. I'm a bit worried about Anthony, that's all. Can you think of any reason he might be upset with you?'

Imogen wondered how to answer. Finally, she came up with a reply.

'I think he's got a bit of a crush on me. I didn't lead him on, Mrs Hewlett. Honestly I didn't.'

'I believe you, Imogen,' said Mrs Hewlett. 'Anthony's such a sensitive boy. There hasn't been much stability in his life. He tends to have . . . infatuations.'

'I'll try to sort things out,' Imogen said.

Mrs Hewlett managed a smile, albeit a thin one.

Infatuation. Is that what you call it, Mum? That's right, the ghost's around as usual. I heard the pair of you discussing me as if I were some impressionable idiot. What right do you have calling this infatuation? How little you know me, thinking it's just some schoolboy crush! Is it so hard to understand that I can feel deeply about somebody? And you, Imogen, you're just a liar. I understand that now.

This isn't about me getting the wrong end of the stick. You don't want anybody knowing about you and him, that's obvious.

He's different, I suppose, the poor tortured soul from a war-torn continent. Ah, diddums! Well, nobody's going to make a fool of me.

Not even you, Imogen.

Anthony was still watching when Imogen dropped a couple of breakfast rolls and some packs of butter and jam in her bag. He looked on intrigued and snapped her in the act.

Having yourself a picnic, Imogen? What, without me? We'll have to see about that.

His interest intensified a few moments later when he saw Imogen reading the newspaper Mickey Wise had left behind on the table. Something about the way she read it, about the fixed, haunted expression in those heart-stopping eyes of hers, hooked his attention. Anthony waited for her to leave the room then stole across to the table.

'Now, why did you find this so interesting?' he wondered out loud as he examined the paper.

Looks like I'll be following you.

A few minutes later, that's exactly what Anthony was doing – following Imogen down Old Lane, the paper still clutched tightly in his fist. His heart fluttered like a captive bird. Excitement eddied through him. He was getting his life back under control.

Imogen turned into Church Street. All the way down the street she was darting glances to left and right, making sure nobody was watching. Anthony had to slip down the side of the church to stay out of sight.

The village hall! Of course!

Once Imogen was inside, Anthony hurried to the hall and listened. He heard the buzz of two voices. Imogen called him Farid. For several moments Anthony examined the article, and then he smiled. Suddenly everything was clear.

Everything.

KIDDINGTON CHRONICLE
August 15

UNDER SIEGE

Kiddington Mosque was the scene of a tense confrontation as we went to press. Three Afghan asylum seekers are reported to have taken refuge in the mosque after their application to stay in the UK was turned down. Police officers are keeping a watching brief at present, but it is widely expected that entry may be forced at any time.

A police spokesman said: 'Seeking to evade a deportation order is illegal. We would request that the three men surrender themselves to the authorities immediately to prevent any further confrontation.'

However, Ibrahim Siddiqui of the county's Council of Mosques has asked the police to show restraint.

'These men are frightened and vulnerable,' he said. 'Any attempt to enter the mosque and arrest them would raise tensions in the Muslim community.'

The town's MP, Sir Richard Gill, called on the police to take firm action however.

'Lawlessness is unacceptable,' he said. 'The police must not be afraid to do their duty. No amount of political correctness can justify the men's actions.'

As we go to press the issue remains unresolved.

Five

Anthony waited outside the hall for five minutes before he plucked up the courage to move closer, to enter Imogen's new world. When he finally pressed the camera lens to the window, he felt his heart turn cold. Farid had Imogen in his arms. His face was pressed into her hair. Anthony stared with hatred as Farid's enormous hands held her head, turning her face towards his. She was a tiny sliver of whiteness in his brown hands, as much a ghost now as Anthony had ever been. To Anthony's flickering eyes Imogen had become no more than a faded reflection of Farid's size and power, his ability to take her from him, his otherness.

But however much it hurt him to see her with Farid, Anthony knew he had to have these shots. It was as if he was taking a knife to his own soul, carving off slices of feeling with each cut of the blade. They were the truth, the deepest, rawest truth he had ever known, and it had to be recorded. They were going to take pride of place in his gallery, a reminder of Imogen's treachery. Anthony fired off shot after shot, and with every one he recorded another image of betrayal as they sat talking, heads close together.

'Imogen,' he murmured and anguish worked its way through him like a corkscrew.

'My Imogen!'

But she would never be his. She belonged to Farid now.

'Imogen!'

Imogen broke off and took a step back.

'I've got to go,' she said. 'Mum and Dad are both at home. They know what time I get in. I can't go on turning up late all the time. They love me, but there are limits even to their trust. If I'm going to be any use to you at all, I've got to at least play the game.'

She glanced round the hall.

'You should be all right,' she said. 'There's the toilet and a washbasin. They haven't cut the water off, have they?'

'No,' said Farid. 'I am able to do my ablutions before prayer. I will need a towel.'

'I can take care of that,' said Imogen.

Farid nodded.

'I don't know what I would have done without you,' he said, any further words stalling in his throat.

Imogen started to go, but he clung to her hand, as if willing the world to be normal.

'Imogen . . .'

'Yes, I know,' she said, interrupting him. 'You need a towel and you want me to call Sophie.'

That wasn't it at all, but he nodded his agreement anyway. She took her mobile from her bag.

'It slipped my mind. I could have done it while I was here.'

Farid smiled.

'I think we were too busy.'

Imogen blushed. Farid was drawing her towards the adult world but she hesitated to enter. She had nothing to be ashamed of. They had only kissed but she had lost herself in their embrace, hardly caring where that warmth, those instincts took her.

133

'Look,' she said, 'I've got to go now, but I won't forget about Sophie. I'll call her on the way home.'

She leaned forward and kissed him.

'I'll let you know what she says when I come back. That'll be when I'm on my way to the Inn.'

'When's that?'

'I'll call in about half-past four. If I don't come, it isn't because I don't want to. It will be because there's somebody around. We can't be too obvious.'

Farid nodded.

'I understand.'

'Same rules for bringing you soap and food. I'll try to bring you something cooked from work, but only if I can slip in here unnoticed.'

She closed her eyes for a moment.

'If I was the one who got you caught,' she said, 'I would never forgive myself.'

To think I loved you!

I would have done everything for you, Imogen. You could have had something good with me, but you chose danger, didn't you?

Well, any feelings I had for you have burned out now, burned to a cinder. All that's left is to pay you back, and believe me, I will. You see, I've got everything I need to take my revenge. It's all here in my camera.

That afternoon Imogen was hurrying down Old Lane. She was flushed and her heart was beating. She had been about to turn left into Chapel Street to deliver Farid the packed lunch she had made him when she heard the throb of an engine. There was a vehicle behind her. It was the minibus that dropped The Boys off every day after work. It had *Kiddington B* emblazoned on the side.

'Fancy a lift, Immy girl?' someone called.

It was Peter Riley. She would have recognised the nasal Liverpool accent anywhere.

'Come on,' he called as the minibus cruised alongside. 'We can squeeze a little one in somewhere.'

I bet you can, Imogen thought, but you're not going to get the chance.

'That's all right, thanks,' she called back with forced cheerfulness. 'I'll be there in a minute.'

She was still hoping she could let them pass out of sight and re-trace her steps to the village hall.

'Don't be stand-offish,' said Mickey Wise. 'Climb aboard.'

Imogen shook her head.

'Honestly,' she said, 'I'd rather walk.'

Imogen left work at her usual time. There was a car with its lights on in the car park. The rain sparkled in the head-lights and the windscreen wipers squeaked against the glass, leaving a smear of grease where one was worn. The driver waved and drove off. Checking that there was nobody else about, she hurried down to Chapel Street and walked quickly through the steady beat of the rain. By the time she reached the village hall she was thoroughly soaked. Giving the street another check, she slipped inside.

'It's me,' she said.

For a couple of beats the only sound was the tick of the rain on the dust-smeared windows. Her heart stuttered.

'Farid?'

Finally he appeared. Imogen was greeted by an unshaven and rather dishevelled Farid. When she reached up to kiss him his clothes smelled of perspiration and a faint musti-ness.

'Thank God!' she said. 'For a moment I thought they'd found you.'

Her eyes drifted towards the window.

'Did something happen?' Farid asked.

Imogen explained about the minibus.

'Here,' she said. 'There are the sandwiches I made earlier on and a chicken salad from the Inn.'

Farid sat in a corner and started eating immediately. Imogen unpacked the other things she had brought: a towel, a flannel, some wipes, a toothbrush and a tube of toothpaste.

'Did you talk to Sophie?' Farid said through a mouthful of food.

'There isn't much news,' Imogen said. 'The committee have sent off a lot of letters – MPs, the press, that sort of thing – but there haven't been any replies yet.'

'Ahmed and Hamid?'

'Nothing new, I'm afraid. It's still a stand-off.'

Farid sighed.

'Maybe it would be better if the police just came,' he said.

'Don't talk like that!' Imogen cried. 'You can't give up.'

'They're not going to give up either, are they?' Farid said. 'They are so powerful and we . . .' His head sagged. 'Imogen, we are nothing.'

Imogen sat on the floor beside him. She took his hand.

'Farid,' she said, 'you mustn't give up hope. You mustn't. Sophie says you have to sit tight. There's going to be a demonstration of support for you outside the mosque.'

Farid nodded, probably for Imogen's benefit. She so wanted to bring him good news.

'I'd like to believe it will do some good,' he said.

'It will,' said Imogen. 'Please believe me. I'll come every day. I'll go on every demonstration. I'll never let you down.'

Farid forced a smile.

'I know,' he said. 'But not all the world is like you.'

As if to prove that fact, outside in the rain a camera clicked through a rain-beaded lens.

The moment Imogen arrived home she was met at the door by her mother.

'What's going on?' Mum demanded, her face taut with suspicion.

'What do you mean?' Imogen said.

'You're half an hour late, and don't tell me you've been working because I called the Hewletts.'

'Oh Mum, you didn't!'

Imogen saw her father hovering in the living-room doorway.

'Yes, Imogen, as a matter of fact I did.' She darted a glare at Dad. 'Your dad may swallow your stories, but not me.'

Imogen decided that attack was the best form of defence.

'Mum, what are you accusing me of?'

'I'm not accusing you of anything,' Mum said. 'I'm simply trying to understand your recent behaviour. It's obvious to me that you've been meeting someone.'

For a moment Imogen was tempted to tell the truth. After all, her parents were bound to be on the side of Farid and his friends. The impulse didn't last long. They were bound to stop her going to the hall. They would never give Farid up – that was against all their instincts – but they would take over from her, do anything to keep her out of trouble. She would be left at home while they took it in turns to drop things off at the hall. Farid's destiny would be taken completely out of her hands. No, the truth was no good.

'OK,' Imogen said, 'you're right, as it happens. I have been seeing someone.'

Mum's eyes narrowed.

'Who?'

Imogen glanced at Dad.

'Who?' Mum repeated, facing down her husband's attempt at an interruption.

Imogen's mind raced through the possibilities before she finally fastened on a name.

'Andy,' she said. 'His name's Andy.'

'I haven't heard you mention any Andy,' Mum said, still not convinced.

'He's an anarchist. He lives in Crofton.'

'You've got a boyfriend?'

'Sort of,' Imogen said, still not quite comfortable with the latest raft of lies. Give them just enough of the truth to keep them happy, she thought. It will be easier to cover up for any mistakes.

'He's in the Refugee Committee. He's keeping me up to date with the campaign, the two men in the mosque.'

It was Dad who picked up on the mistake.

'Two?'

'I beg your pardon?'

'I thought there were three of them.'

Lamely, Imogen stammered an answer.

'Isn't that what I said?'

To her relief, the moment passed.

It was just after nine o'clock that night when Imogen heard a knock on her bedroom door. It was Dad.

'Can I come in?' Dad asked.

'Sure.'

She gave him a guarded look.

'This isn't another lecture, is it?'

'No, not at all. Your mum didn't mean to get all heavy earlier.'

Imogen smiled. She could hear the old hippie in his words.

'If that's not being heavy, I'd hate to see her when she loses her temper,' Imogen said.

'Why didn't you talk to us?' Dad said. 'You must have known we'd be cool with a boyfriend.'

Imogen rolled her eyes.

'Now, that isn't fair,' Dad said. 'We're hardly ogres. Why all the secrecy?'

'Oh Dad, did you tell your parents everything?'

Dad's eyes met hers.

'I see your point.'

But he wasn't entirely satisfied. There was one more question.

'Just one thing,' he said. 'What's with the food?'

Imogen's skin prickled.

'Sorry?'

'The food, Imogen. I'm not stupid.'

'Andy comes over on his bike,' Imogen said hurriedly. 'It's a kind of picnic.'

Dad arched an eyebrow.

'What? At seven in the morning?'

'He calls in on his way to Kiddington,' Imogen insisted. 'He's there most of the day, helping with the campaign. I'd be there too, but for the job.'

Dad's eyes were still cloudy with suspicion.

'Look, love,' he said by way of a parting shot, 'tell me something. You and your mum may think I'm a soft touch, but even I've got my limits. Talk to me.'

Even now Imogen couldn't bring herself to tell him the truth. If she did, she might have to face not seeing Farid again.

'OK,' she said, moving deeper through her forest of lies. 'It's like this. Andy's parents don't like him getting involved in politics. They had a row.'

There was a moment's hesitation, then she added, 'He stayed out all night.'

The story was meant to contain just enough danger to sucker Dad. The look in his eyes told her he'd swallowed the story.

'Where did he stay?'

Imogen's mind buzzed with questions. Tell the truth? Mention the village hall? No, that was way too risky.

'There's a storeroom at the Inn.'

'Oh Imogen, you silly girl!'

He turned her story over in his mind.

'There's nothing else I need to know, is there?'

Imogen got his drift.

'No, Dad,' she said. 'Nothing like that. I'm not stupid.'

Dad nodded grimly.

'Glad to hear it. OK, love, I believe you, but this has to stop.'

'No problem, Dad,' she replied, swimming through the lies. 'Andy's already getting it sorted. He's gone home to patch it up with his parents.'

'And that really is the lot?' Dad asked. 'There's nothing else to come back and bite us?'

Imogen took a deep breath.

'Nothing,' she said.

Six

The next few days were tough for Imogen. She could only risk one visit a day to the village hall, and that had to be for a maximum of ten minutes. In an effort to keep her parents off the scent, she had said she wasn't going to see Andy until the Refugee Committee's evening vigil outside the mosque at the end of the week. One of her worst moments was when she had to explain her story to Andy over the phone. He had to be warned, of course.

The evening of the vigil, Imogen called on Farid on her way home from the Inn.

'How are you holding up?' she asked.

Farid stared back. His eyes were dull and shadowed. He was weary from the long days of waiting. Three books lay on the floor of the tiny kitchen together with a couple of newspapers. The stand-off at the mosque had slipped from the headlines and was now relegated to a paragraph on the inside pages.

'Somebody nearly saw me today,' he said.

'What!'

'A couple of boys were playing football, hitting the ball against the wall. One of them came right up to the window.'

'But he didn't see you, did he?'

Farid's brow furrowed.

'I can't be sure.'

Imogen brought the fingers of one hand to her lips.

'Try to think, Farid,' she said. 'This is important.'

'Imogen,' he answered, 'I've thought of little else. I just don't know.'

She took his hands.

'I don't suppose there's anything we can do, anyway,' she said. 'Look, I've got to go. I daren't let my parents get suspicious again. I think they swallowed the Andy story.'

Farid's dark eyes looked troubled.

'I don't like all this lying,' he said. 'Especially not about other boys.'

'Farid,' she said, 'you can be so silly sometimes. Don't be jealous because of a made-up story!'

He nodded reluctantly and she kissed him.

'I'm going to the vigil tonight,' she said. 'I'll bring you any news tomorrow.'

As she slipped out of the hall she saw Farid sitting slumped in a corner, misery showing in his hunched shoulders, his head resting on his knees. The sight ripped right through her.

Mum watched Imogen closely as she walked from the front door to the foot of the stairs.

'What?' Imogen asked.

She couldn't believe the way Mum was carrying on. All that stuff about the carefree days of the Seventies, and here she was, Marsham's answer to Big Brother. What next, electronic tagging?

'Are you still planning to go to the vigil?' Mum asked.

'Yes, Kes is giving me a lift.'

'No need for that,' said Mum. 'Your dad and I are going.'

Imogen exhaled impatiently.

'Is this because of Andy?' she asked.

'Not at all,' Mum said. 'Our beliefs haven't changed, you know.'

Imogen nodded, though she wasn't convinced that was the real reason.

'We'll be leaving in about half an hour,' Mum said.

'So I've got time for a shower first?'

'Plenty of time.'

Imogen stood under the shower-head, letting the hot spray play on her face. She wanted to wash everything away: the worry about Farid, the confusion about her feelings, the relentless teasing of The Boys, the sense that everything was spinning out of control. In her mind's eye she was juggling shards of glass, being cut to ribbons by all the lies she was having to tell. Then there was Anthony – how she wanted to rinse away his accusing stare! She had bumped into him on her way into the Inn that afternoon. She had tried to speak to him, just as Mrs Hewlett had asked, but he hadn't said a word in return. Instead he had looked right back at her, hostility flashing in his flickering blue eyes, as though she had done him some great injury.

When she stepped out of the shower, wrapping a towel round her, she heard Mum calling up.

'I've rung Kes,' she said. 'I told him there was no need to give you a lift.'

'OK.'

Imogen rubbed the condensation from the mirror in the bathroom cabinet and looked at herself.

'This is getting out of hand,' she murmured.

'Good turn-out,' Dad remarked, looking around the fifty or so demonstrators drawn up behind police barriers opposite the mosque.

'Yes,' Imogen said. 'Not bad, but over half the crowd is from the Muslim community.'

It was true. Most of the white faces belonged to activists

from the Refugee Committee. There was no doubt what it meant: they were losing the argument among the white people in the town. A few motorists said as much, shouting insults through their open windows.

'Here's Sophie,' Mum said.

Sophie was handing out candles for the vigil, lighting them as she went. The flames guttered briefly then illuminated the demonstrators' faces.

'Is Andy here yet?' Mum asked.

Imogen searched Sophie's face. What if Kes hadn't passed on her cover story? But he had.

'He's always late,' Sophie said. 'It's part of being an anarchist. He's not a bit like you, Imogen. I don't know what you see in him.'

Imogen managed a half-smile. Sophie was trying just a bit too hard to convince.

'Any response to the letter-writing campaign?' she asked, keen to change the subject.

'Not much,' said Sophie. 'We've had support from a few trade union branches and some individuals. Nothing from the MPs yet though.'

Even the usually irrepressible Sophie sounded pessimistic.

'It doesn't look good. The police are trying to get an injunction. They could go into the mosque any time.'

'What are their chances?' Imogen asked.

Sophie shrugged. 'Beats me.'

Which meant: not good.

'Hey,' Sophie said, 'there's Andy.'

Wincing inside, Imogen introduced him to her parents. She'd forgotten quite how unappealing he looked. She saw Mum running her gaze over his greasy combat jacket, faded jeans and black workmen's boots. The missing eyebrow got a particularly long examination. Finally, Imogen made an excuse and dragged Andy to the other end of the vigil.

'Sorry to lumber you with this,' she said, 'but I had to come up with something.'

'No sweat,' said Andy. 'Anything for a mate. You don't want us to hug or anything, do you? You know, make it convincing?'

Imogen grimaced.

'Don't even think about it.'

'Fair enough,' said Andy, giving her a mischievous wink. 'Just a thought.'

The protestors started chanting their support for the asylum seekers. Imogen heard the Town Hall clock strike the hour. Ninety minutes and she could go home.

'So that's Andy,' Dad said.

Imogen heard something in his voice. Mum always prided herself on knowing Imogen inside out, but it was Dad who really picked things up, and he had clearly picked something up at the vigil.

'He's a real charmer, isn't he?' Mum said, heavy on the irony.

'Now now, Karen,' Dad said. 'Don't go making on-the-spot judgements. You don't know the lad.'

Imogen flashed an unspoken thank you his way. Mum was right though. Andy had all the charm of swamp rat. He was turning out to be an embarrassing choice of alibi.

'I know his type,' said Mum. 'I've met a few in my time, though I never went out with anyone who was missing an eyebrow.'

'I didn't say it was serious,' Imogen protested.

'Just a *sort of* boyfriend, eh?' Dad said, catching her eye in the rear-view mirror.

His tone of voice made Imogen's skin prickle. He knew more than he was letting on. Imogen looked away.

All night long the rain came down, hissing through the echoey woods, stirring the drenching darkness into a black, raging stew. Outside her warm bedroom the night wind shrieked.

And Imogen thought of Farid.

Farid too was at his window. At night he felt safe enough to come to the glass and watch the late summer storm. There would be nobody venturing down Chapel Street in the drumming rain. The flashes of lightning left images printed in front of his eyes, like viewing the world as a negative. He thought of the battles that had raged long ago in these woods and he thought of the battles that were being fought over his future. Why did he have to meet somebody like Imogen at a time like this, in the middle of these events? He reached out his arms in a gesture of despair. His hand caught a bottle and it tumbled to the floor. He looked down at the fragments of glass and saw broken dreams.

At the Inn Imogen was serving the Friday morning breakfasts. The Boys were quizzing her about the vigil.

'Have you seen your picture in the paper?' Wise asked.

She was shown standing next to Andy, their faces illuminated by candlelight.

'Nice,' said Wise. 'Really romantic. So this is the boyfriend.'

'No,' Imogen said. Then she thought of her parents. 'Well, sort of.'

'And you both want these scroungers coming from all over the world,' Wise said coldly, 'taking what we've worked all our lives for?'

'Mr Wise,' Imogen said, struggling to keep hold of her temper, 'they're not scroungers. They're refugees.'

'Sure,' Riley joined in, 'so they say.'

'No,' Imogen said. 'You don't understand. I've met these men. They just want to make a new life.'

'Exactly,' said Wise. 'At our expense. Listen to me, darling – when you've lived a little, you'll change your tune. You'll want to keep the money you earn instead of giving it to some self-appointed refugee.'

Imogen was about to continue the discussion when Mr Hewlett came over. 'Table four needs you,' he said.

Imogen heard Hewlett asking The Boys if they wouldn't mind passing on the breakfast-table politics. He wasn't exactly making a stand but she felt grateful for his intervention.

Imogen got home about ten-past nine. She hadn't noticed Anthony following. She walked into the house still smarting from The Boys' words. Dad was making coffee in the kitchen.

'What's wrong?' she asked, seeing the expression on his face.

'It's just been on the news,' he said. 'The police have gone into the mosque.'

'Oh no!'

Panic shuddered through her. Any time now all her lies were going to come home to roost.

'I'll bring it up on Teletext.'

At that moment the phone rang and Dad went to answer it. Alone in the room, Imogen read the news item.

Newsflash, it read. *At eight thirty this morning Kiddington police forced entry into the town's mosque and arrested the occupants. The men, both in their twenties, are asylum seekers. They took refuge in the mosque in protest at a deportation order.*

Through the lens of his camera, Anthony caught the moment when Imogen turned desperately in the direction of the village hall. The expression in her eyes was close to terror.

Seven

Sunday evening would be difficult for many people. Ahmed and Hamid would sit it out in a cell at Heathrow, waiting to be flown out of the country back to Germany, the first European country in which they had sought refuge. The officer in charge of the police operation would have to explain to the waiting press pack why they had two, and not all three, illegal immigrants in custody. In the following week's *Kiddington Chronicle* there would be a cartoon depicting a confused-looking policeman, with the caption: *One of our immigrants is missing.* Imogen would wriggle and squirm uneasily while Dad, always waiting until Mum had left the room, interrogated her in whispers about the identity of the real boyfriend. He knew, of course, all but knew for certain, but he had no proof.

For Farid it was the hardest time of all. The sequence of events that would put his life in danger had begun about three o'clock. He had been dozing fitfully, wondering when Imogen would come again, when he heard voices. He looked out through the rain-spotted window panes and saw the two boys, the ones who had been playing football against the walls of the building. This time there was no football. It didn't take a genius to work out why they were there. They'd spotted him all right when they collected their football that time and, in that conspiratorial way young boys have, they were trying to work out what to do with the information. Farid watched them staring at the village hall. They didn't take their eyes off it. One thing he knew for sure – as far as this hiding place went, the game was up.

'Imogen,' he murmured. 'I need you. I need you now.'

But Imogen was unable to call in on him. Dad was visiting a university colleague in Crofton. He offered Imogen a lift to the Inn.

'That's all right, Dad,' she said. 'I don't want you going out of your way just for me.'

'I won't be going out of my way,' said Dad, his eyes looking into her, his suspicion strong enough to lift a truck. 'I just have to hang a left at the top of Slaughter Lane and I'm back on the main road.'

Hang a left! Imogen wrinkled her nose. Honestly, Dad and his American crime novels!

Reluctantly, she pulled on her jacket. She was aware of the food she had packed in her shoulder bag. It was getting harder and harder to get to Farid. Her heartbeat accelerated. It was that feeling she'd had the day of the picnic – that she had abandoned him.

As soon as the boys had gone Farid let himself out through the fire exit. Pulling the hood of his sweatshirt over his head he jogged to the end of Chapel Street and into Old Lane. His mind was racing. How would Imogen find him? Would she make the connections? Then he thought of Ahmed and Hamid and wondered where they were now. Still in the UK? On an aeroplane bound for . . . what? Another detention centre, or even back to Afghanistan?

To Farid at that moment his whole future was a vortex of darkness, sucking the world dry of hope, of love, of dreams. Something was snapping inside him. In the hostels and detention centres he had seen people start to slide into blank despair because of much smaller obstacles than the ones he faced now. He had watched their eyes go dead as they realised journey's end was a wasteland. Was he next?

He looked the possibility in the face then shook his head in a deliberate gesture of dismissal. Win or lose, at least he would fight.

He had a hiding place in mind.

It was ten past seven before Imogen got away from the Inn. It was The Boys' fault. They hadn't seen her for two days and they had a lot of teasing to catch up on.

As she hurried down Old Lane, she heard footsteps. She looked around but the lane was deserted. Not for the first time she had the feeling she wasn't alone. She imagined Farid hunched in a corner, hungry and miserable, waiting for her. She had to be strong for him.

As she turned into Chapel Street and approached the church, her heart juddered. There was a police car pulled up in the driveway of St Thomas's Church. Across the road from the parish hall there was a second police vehicle – a white van. She saw a well-dressed woman in her thirties, armed with a spiral-bound notepad.

'What's going on?' Imogen asked.

The reporter looked at her as if she'd just popped her head out of the drains.

'The police,' Imogen said, refusing to be ignored. 'What are they here for?'

The reporter sighed.

'You'll see it on the TV news,' she said. 'If you must know, it's the asylum seeker, the one who got away from Kiddington Mosque. Two boys say he was here.'

Imogen's skin prickled.

'Did they catch him?'

A shake of the head.

'No, he's done a bunk. They've found food wrappers though. Somebody's been helping him by the look of it. That could be a good story in its own right.'

Imogen stared back, feeling as though she was being lowered gradually into a deep pit, into the waiting dark beneath.

'Anyway,' the reporter said, 'I've got things to do.'

Imogen nodded, then called after the woman.

'Thank you,' she said, without really meaning it.

Imogen was caught in an agony of indecision. Go home – that was the logical thing, the only sane thing she could do. But that would mean leaving Farid out there, lost and alone. No, somehow he had got out before the police came. He wasn't giving up, so why should she? But what could she do?

A voice broke in on her thoughts.

'Looking for someone?'

It was Anthony.

'No, I—'

'There's no use pretending, Imogen. I know.'

She turned startled eyes in his direction.

'You don't think it's going to work out, do you? It's almost over.'

Imogen had had enough of Anthony's strange ways.

'Oh, do go away,' she said. 'I'm not in the mood.'

'You can't get rid of me that easily,' said Anthony. 'You'll always be with me, even when you're not here.'

At his words, Imogen stared in disbelief.

Anthony gave his parting shot.

'I'm always going to be with you.'

It took Imogen a few moments to gather her thoughts. Immediately they returned to Farid. Without her, he had nothing – no money, no food, and no connection with the outside world. She rummaged for her mobile phone.

'Sophie? It's me, Imogen. Look, the police are on to Farid. What? No, they didn't catch him. Somehow he got out of the village hall before the raid. No, I've no idea where he is.'

But that wasn't true. Even while she was speaking, Imogen's mind filled with the sights and sounds of New Pool. She remembered a sunset she had spent talking to Farid there. Of course! The boathouse. Where else was he going to be? He didn't know anyone in Marsham. It was the only shelter available to him.

'Sophie, I've just got it. I know where he is.'

Without another word of explanation, she hung up. Dad would be waiting for her. He was bound to have rumbled her now. But what could she do? Farid needed her. Whatever the consequences, she had to go to him.

Go to him she did, but if she had glanced behind her she would have seen a figure, pale and shadowy, a ghost boy who was determined to haunt her. Imogen raced along the lakeside path while, in the bracken, Anthony followed at a distance.

She raced to the boathouse.

Snap!

Alerted by her voice, Farid came to the door.

Snap!

Briefly, they embraced.

Snap!

And went inside.

Mum was anxious.

'Tim,' she said, 'I think you should phone the Hewletts.'

'I already have,' he said.

'So where is she?'

Dad looked away. The way he did it rang alarm bells.

'Tim? Tim, talk to me. You know something, don't you?'

The admission, when it came, was bleak and subdued.

'Karen, I think I know where she is.'

Mum stared at her husband as if he had betrayed her.

'Go on, where?' said Mum.

Dad still couldn't meet her eyes.

'I'm pretty sure she's been taking food to this boy.'

He finally turned to look at her.

'Wherever she is, she'll be with him.'

When Anthony arrived home he ran up to his room. The image of Imogen and Farid embracing was still in his mind. He opened his bedroom door and started. Mum was waiting for him.

'Where have you been?' she asked.

'Nowhere.'

Mum snorted. 'You spend a lot of time there, don't you?'

'What's this about?' Anthony asked, ignoring the sarcasm.

'I know you're following Imogen,' she explained. 'Anthony, this has got to stop.'

'I don't know what you mean.'

Mum reached for his hand and walked him to the gallery. She pointed to the photographs.

'Anthony, I used to think this was harmless. But now . . .' She shook her head. 'It's an obsession.'

Anthony protested immediately.

'You're exaggerating.'

'No, Anthony,' said Mum. 'No, I'm not.'

Her voice softened.

'Anthony, sit down. Please.'

He stared at her for a moment but did as he was told.

'I've let this go on too long. You're going to hear me out.

This might be hard to take, Anthony, but Imogen isn't interested in you.'

Anthony made to get up.

'No, hear me out.' She waited a beat. 'Imogen didn't want to hurt you. She really didn't. Whatever you think she's done to you, it isn't true. You're her friend. That's all you're ever going to be.'

Anthony tried to get up but Mum held on.

'No, you're not walking away and I'm not going to let you carry on living in a dream world. Listen, Anthony, I'm telling you this because I love you more than anything in the world. You think I wasn't there for you when you were younger. Maybe that's true. Maybe I was weak. I don't know. But I will never put anyone before you. Never! You've been hurt, but not by Imogen. Blame me if you want, but not Imogen. Accept her for what she is – your friend.'

At long last she let go of his hands.

'Think about it.'

Anthony did think about it. For the next few hours he thought about nothing else. His hands burned where Mum had held them. It was as if she had branded truth into the palms. The soft flesh burned with shame. How could he have read Imogen so wrong? How could he have been so blind, so stupid, so utterly, unforgivably weak and needy? Nor was Imogen the only person he had let down. There was Mum too. All these years he had given her hell for siding with Dad. He was just beginning to realise: there's only one person Mum is siding with.

Me.

Imogen swung the chains that hung from the overhead timbers and inspected the roof dubiously.

'Are you sure this will keep the rain off?' she said.

Farid shrugged.

'The floor seems dry,' he said. 'I'll be fine.'

'I just wish there was a lock on the door,' Imogen said. 'Something to keep people out.'

'Do you really think I need a lock?' Farid asked. 'The lake doesn't seem to attract many visitors.'

'It's not as though there's much either of us can do,' Imogen said. 'I'll keep my fingers crossed for you.'

Farid raised her hand to his lips and kissed her fingertips.

'This kiss is for luck,' he said.

Her throat was flushed with colour. She took a shuddering breath.

'I'm not looking forward to going home,' she said. 'Mum and Dad will be hopping mad.'

'What will you tell them?' Farid asked, letting her hand slip away from him.

'The truth,' Imogen said. 'I think I owe them that.'

Farid nodded.

'I think it's for the best.'

He watched her hurrying along the path towards Battle Lane. He didn't notice the car headlights being extinguished just beyond the screen of trees.

Long after Mum had left Anthony worked stubbornly on the latest batch of photographs. He developed them. He pegged them up, winced as he did it, barely able to look at them. Everything he did he did like an automaton. He went through the motions. It still hurt to see Imogen in Farid's arms.

When he had finished, he left the dark room and walked over to the window. From there he could see down as far as Slaughter Lane. All those grand ideas of mine! he thought. All those dreams of Imogen! Who was I kidding? It was all a stupid fantasy.

At that moment Anthony felt as if he was emerging from a deep sleep.

*

Imogen was almost at the road now. Around her, shadows were springing up, seeping from the darkening woods. The last rays of the sun slanted between the trees and fell on the surface of the lake.

'I don't know how to do this,' she murmured to herself. 'What do I tell them?'

It wouldn't be too hard with Dad. He half-knew already. Mum was the problem. She would go ballistic.

'Come on, Imogen,' she told herself. 'You can do this. You've got to.'

Then she heard something.

'Who's there?' she asked, trying to disguise the quiver in her voice.

A crow-flutter of fright filled her chest. She had heard heavy footsteps, a man's footsteps.

'Who's there?' she asked. 'Farid?'

But she knew it wasn't him. She could hear the man's breathing. Fear trickled down her spine.

Then a wild guess, more in hope than conviction.

'Anthony?'

She wanted it to be him. Odd he might be, but he was harmless.

The figure that stepped out of the shadows wasn't either of them. Imogen's features relaxed nevertheless.

'Do you know you've just scared me witless?' she said. 'Honestly, what are you doing creeping round the woods?'

The man didn't answer. She saw his eyes. They seemed hard, shrunk to ice-blue points in his face. What's more, the face was a mask. There was no expression – just darkness, a smoky menace that seemed to have crept in from the woods.

'Is something the matter?' she asked. 'What's the matter?'

The fear that evaporated on seeing him returned. She felt his hand on her wrist and started to struggle. A flash of fright lit her eyes.

'What are you doing?' she asked, her voice stripped down to a thin tissue of fear. 'Please don't.'

But he was tugging at her, pulling her off the path.

'No!'

Instinctively, more in alarm than anger, she raked her fingernails down his arm. Feeling his hands relax round her wrist, she pulled away and ran, stumbling through the bracken. It snapped against her bare legs, splashing them with the gathered raindrops. Twigs flicked in her face, tugged at her sleeves. Her hair was plastered against her skull.

Help me!

Then the thought became words.

'Help me!' she cried.

She stumbled on to Battle Lane. The bridge over the old disused railway line was ahead of her and, beyond that, the lights of Old Marsham Inn.

'Please help me!' she sobbed.

But there was nobody to help her. The gathering gloom hung in the woods like a black curtain and the trees looked on in dumb witness. Nobody heard. Imogen hadn't even reached the bridge when his car skidded in front of her. He got out and she backed away. She shrivelled under his gaze. His ice-blue eyes.

'No,' she said. 'Don't hurt me. It's me, Imogen. What have I ever done to you? I thought we were friends.'

He made a grab for her but she wriggled free and ran. She got as far as the bridge before his hands clamped her arms to her sides. Again, feeling his breath on her face, she cried out. Sweat was oozing from every pore. She could feel the fabric of her top sticking to her back.

'Leave me alone!' she yelled, her whole body straining to fight back.

She pulled her arm free of his grip and tried to hit him but he was too strong. His hands went round her throat, his weight and the urgency of his grasp pushing her back until she could feel the low stone wall of the bridge against the back of her knees.

'Please,' she cried. 'Just stop!'

Then he spoke.

'No,' he said. 'You don't want me to stop, do you? That's not what you really mean.'

Imogen's eyes widened in horror.

'Start being honest with yourself, Imogen. I've watched you flaunting yourself. You always wanted to be the centre of attention, didn't you? You wanted me to look at you. Why else would you dress the way you did?'

Imogen's face twisted in revulsion.

'Stop it!' she said. 'You're sick!'

She struggled to be free, but his grip was like steel. She had no choice but to listen. His words were razor cuts in the veil of terror that shrouded her.

'No, just sick of waiting. Looking at you. But that isn't enough any more. Now I want you. You're mine, Imogen, the way it was always going to be.'

The wind blew around her, gusts like hornets buzzing with anger. His fingers were on her throat, digging into the pressure points either side of her neck. The world began to swim before her eyes. She entered another continent where there were no worries about parents, no anxieties about Farid – just a hinterland of terror and disgust. One last time she lashed feebly against him, desperate to be free, putting everything into a last act of resistance.

'Stop!'

Then she lost her footing and toppled backwards over the stone wall. As she tumbled into space her startled cry lingered in the man's ear.

In the boathouse Farid heard a car engine. He didn't pay it much attention, just as he had dismissed a sound earlier. He had thought for a moment that it was a cry, but it was more likely the shriek of a night bird. He thought of Imogen, let her face flood into his mind, smiled and looked out at the lake. Her presence in the world helped lessen his fear.

But for Imogen terror was complete. In the tangle of briars and undergrowth under Old Lane Bridge she was fighting against the night as it closed round her like a gauntlet.

'Help me!' she croaked, and wondered why the words stalled in her throat.

Then she heard him crashing about in the undergrowth and she was silent. Hurt and broken as she was, she tried to press her body into the earth where he couldn't see her. She felt the vibration of his footsteps in the ground and waited.

'Imogen!' he hissed, afraid to speak louder in case he drew somebody's attention.

A car drove down Slaughter Lane and he cursed. Giving the tangle of bracken, nettles and thistles a last look, he scrambled up the slope to his car.

The smell of the earth and of her own blood seeped into her mind. The taste in her mouth was sour and cloying. Then Imogen slipped away from the world and black was the night.

NEWS REPORT
Tuesday, August 19, 6 a.m.

MEDLON RADIO NEWS

First up, a Marsham girl, Imogen Bayliss, is causing concern. Imogen, sixteen, disappeared after leaving work at a local hotel on Sunday evening. Her anxious parents say she has never stayed away from home overnight before without letting them know first, and that her disappearance is completely out of character. Police have contacted Imogen's friends and have started a search of the area.

Police sources say there may be a link with the disappearance of a young asylum seeker who has been served a deportation order. They are known to have met. The missing refugee, Farid Abdullah, aged eighteen, has evaded police on two occasions, first when they controversially broke into Kiddington Mosque and, most recently, when they raided Marsham village hall on a tip-off. A police spokesman has told MRN that they have no leads as to his whereabouts. Two other men were deported from the country last night.

Now sport. Kiddington Harriers have snatched central defender Jimmy Tobin from under the noses of rivals Medlon United. Medlon were expected to play Tobin in their opener this Saturday but the promising 20-year-old will now play in Kiddington colours.

Eight

Tim and Karen Bayliss listened to the news and exchanged glances across the kitchen table.

'Do you think they're together?' said Mum, her face picked clean of colour.

They both looked derelict from lack of sleep.

'I wish I knew.'

Dad reached out and took his wife's hand.

'What time does the search start again?'

'Seven o'clock.'

'Tim, what if . . .?'

Dad faced down the nightmare in his wife's eyes.

'No, she's with this Farid boy,' he said. 'She's got to be.'

'If something has happened to her . . .'

Tears spilled down her cheeks.

'Tim, how could we go on?'

Farid had returned to the boathouse about two o'clock that morning and snatched a little fitful sleep. From the undergrowth he had watched the police going over the boathouse with a fine-toothed comb. Hour after hour he had watched police officers and lines of villagers moving through the dripping darkness. He had seen them going through the woods, beating at the undergrowth with their sticks. Late into the evening their flashlights had raked the trees and bracken. *All this for one frightened refugee,* Farid thought – *one hungry, half-broken lost boy. How they must hate us being here!*

Twice he had almost been discovered and twice he had stumbled away, heart thudding in his rib cage as his mind reeled with the force of their hatred.

Now, as the bleary light of a showery, late summer morning filtered through the woods, Farid hugged himself and prepared for another day as a hunted fugitive.

If they think you've run off with him, why are they beating the woods?

Do they know something? Has he hurt you? Is that it?

Where are you, Imogen?

What's he done to you?

Imogen was also the subject of conversation over the breakfast table at Old Marsham Inn.

'I knew she was a bit of an innocent,' Barry Hewlett said, having to serve the guests in her place. 'Head full of romantic notions. But I wouldn't have had her down as an absconder. She seemed quite a responsible young girl. Honestly, running off with some rootless refugee at sixteen! Her parents must be devastated.'

'If she was mine,' Mickey Wise said, 'I'd throttle her.'

Gordon Craig started.

'Not literally, Professor,' Wise said, seeing the abrupt change of expression, 'but I'd teach her a lesson she'd never forget.'

For once, Peter Riley disagreed.

'Behave yourselves,' he said. 'Weren't you ever young? She's gone off on an adventure. Poor little cow thinks she's in love. She'll soon come home, a little older and wiser.'

'Yes,' said Wise. 'Or pregnant. Have you thought of that?'

Craig finally spoke.

'She wouldn't do that,' he said. 'Not Imogen.'

'Wouldn't she?' said Wise. 'Young girls these days, I wouldn't put anything past them.'

'There's one thing you haven't mentioned, gentlemen,' Mrs Hewlett said, arriving with the toast. 'What if she's out there, hurt or . . .'

Her voice started to break. Her eyes flicked round the four men as if they were the most stupid creatures on the planet.

'Don't you see? The police can't be searching the woods for nothing.'

The dining room fell silent. Nobody even exchanged glances.

The news came through at eleven o'clock that morning. A young PC rushed to find Dad.

'Mr Bayliss,' he said, 'we've found her. We've found Imogen.'

All the blue fell from the morning sky and Dad stared with blank eyes.

'Sir, your daughter has been found in undergrowth by Battle Lane Bridge.'

The PC was feeling uncomfortable.

'Mr Bayliss,' he said, 'did you hear me?'

Then for the first time Dad reacted. A tearless cry erupted from him and for a moment, he staggered against the PC. Moments later a stunned and ashen Tim Bayliss was being led to a police car.

It was five o'clock before Anthony heard the news. At the sound of Imogen's name he put down the book he was reading, a second-hand copy of *Wuthering Heights*, and stared at the multi-media centre in the corner of his room. The air seemed to rush from the room. The brutal words of the broadcast pulsated through his mind:

'. . . Marsham girl found among undergrowth . . .'

'. . . exposure . . .'

'. . . has suffered broken ribs and a fractured skull . . .'

'. . . in a coma . . .'

'. . . critically ill . . .'

Anthony looked up and saw a butterfly fluttering outside his window, sunlight illuminating the tiny veins in its wings.

'Imogen!' he groaned. 'My Imogen.'

He walked into the dark room and looked along the gallery. He saw the images of Imogen in Farid's arms, Imogen's tiny head in his huge hands.

'Why did he have to hurt her?' Anthony sobbed, thinking of Imogen in her hospital bed, her fragile life punctuated by the electronic rhythms of a heartbeat monitor. 'Why did he do it?'

He pulled down three photographs. He had to show them to somebody.

Five minutes later a tearful Anthony was in Reception. The photographs were spread out in front of him. In his right hand he was holding the phone. At the sound of footsteps, he looked up. It was Gordon Craig.

'You haven't seen my mum, have you?' Anthony asked. 'There's something I've got to tell her.'

'No, I haven't seen anyone yet. Are you all right, son?'

Anthony shook his head.

'I've got to call the police.'

'Why do you have to do that, son?'

'Because I know.'

'What do you know?'

'I know who hurt Imogen.'

Craig's eyes fell on the photographs.

'Good God!'

He stared at the prints.

'Where did you get these?'

'I took them. I followed them and took pictures.'

'And what did you see? This is important.'

'Them,' Anthony answered. 'Them together.'

Wise and Riley came down the stairs.

'Mickey, Peter,' Craig said. 'Have you seen this lot?'

One picture in particular caught their attention, of Imogen's face framed in Farid's hands, as if he were crushing her skull.

'Jeez!' said Wise. 'Where'd you get them?'

Craig nodded in Anthony's direction.

'We've got the killer,' he said. 'Look what he's doing to her.'

'We should go to the police,' said Wise.

'I was phoning the police,' Anthony said, finding his voice.

'And what are they going to do?' said Riley. 'Give him a slap on the wrist? We should go and give him a taste of British justice. I just wish I knew where he was.'

'I know,' said Craig. 'I recognise the boathouse in the picture. I know where it is.'

'That's it then,' said Riley. 'Let's go get him.'

'Are you up for this, Gordon?' Wise said.

'What do you think?' Craig said. 'That little girl's dying, and what's he going to get for it? He'll be out in a couple of years and she'll be dead. I'm with Peter.'

Wise stared in disbelief.

'Is this the same Prof?'

'This is me,' said Craig. 'Whose side are you on, Mickey?'

There they go.

I've found a way to get justice for Imogen. She's my

friend. I can't help her myself, but they can. They'll find him and do what they have to.

I hope they make him suffer.

Farid had crept back to the boathouse. After a fine late afternoon it was threatening rain again. He ducked under the heavy chains that hung from the ceiling and gulped the contents of a can of Coke he'd found on a fencepost in the woods. The liquid was warm and flat, but it was sweet and it quenched his thirst. All he needed now was something to eat. He felt sick with hunger. His body trembled with it. Why didn't Imogen come? Was something wrong? Was something stopping her coming to him?

He imagined the light dancing in her hazel eyes, her voice on the wind, but the only sound was the jangle of the chains like heavy wind chimes.

Craig was leading the way down Old Lane.

'How do you know where to go?' Wise asked.

'I come walking down here sometimes,' said Craig.

'Pity you didn't come across young Imogen on Sunday night,' said Riley.

They reached the bridge where it had happened. There was a small crowd of inquisitive onlookers and a TV film crew. Two PCs were on duty to keep people away from the crime scene.

'Maybe we should report what we know,' Wise said, suddenly no longer the leader of the gang.

'What?' Craig retorted, his face purple with anger, 'And let him get away with a couple of years in prison? What's he going to get, Mickey? The do-gooders and liberals will let him off with manslaughter, you know that. How many times have you said they should bring back the rope? This way we give him a taste of his own medicine before we hand him over. We'll say he was struggling. We had to restrain him. Nobody will blame us. They'll thank us.'

Wise was wavering. All the times he had ridiculed the quiet Professor and now he was scared by him.

'Come on,' Craig said, his anger hard like falling stones, 'it's what he deserves, isn't it?'

'That's right Mickey,' Riley said. 'What if it was your kid?'

Finally Wise nodded. The three men left the road and entered the woods.

Anthony stepped away from the window. He was trembling. He was aware of his own power, the way Pandora must have been when she opened her box. It was an odd feeling. He was hiding from the world in the familiar surroundings of his gallery.

'I did this for you, Imogen,' he said.

He looked at the photographs, at golden Imogen and her tall, rangy attacker. Looking at Farid now, Anthony was reminded of a wolf. Finally he looked at The Boys, his avenging angels.

Five miles away at Kiddington General Tim Bayliss had brought his wife a coffee from the vending machine in the corridor. She declined with a shake of the head.

'Tim, look at her.'

They stared at Imogen through a window. Her face was bruised and encased in white. An IV rack stood by the bed and a bag of clear liquid hung from it. She was hooked up to machines. A nurse was reading from a clipboard.

'Karen,' said Dad, 'here's the doctor.'

They looked expectantly in his direction.

'What can you tell us?' Mum asked.

'We'll be taking her down to theatre,' the doctor said. 'We'll know more once we've taken a proper look at the head injury. Your daughter is very poorly, I'm afraid. There are the injuries, then there is the time she has spent out in the elements. I will be able to give you a better assessment in a few hours.'

Dad watched Mum staring through the window and slipped his arm round her shoulder.

Anthony was about to close the door to the dark room when something caught his eye. Patterns of fright eddied across his skin.

'No, it can't be!'

He snatched his magnifier from its shelf and examined the photograph of Imogen and Farid embracing. Over to the left of the shot, in the right-hand corner, there were two tiny lights. Frowning, Anthony walked over to the line where other prints were hanging. He seized one of the better exposures.

'Oh no!'

He stared at his portraits of The Boys. In one Craig was getting out of his car. Anthony's eyes flicked back to the photograph of Farid and Imogen. There was no doubt about it. That afternoon, just before the attack, a green Hillman Imp had been parked on Battle Lane, its headlights gleaming.

Craig stood by the lakeside.

'That's the boathouse,' he said.

'Look, lads,' Wise said, 'I don't know about this.'

'Getting cold feet, Mickey?' Riley said. 'Tell you what, if you haven't got the belly for it, why don't you go back to the Inn?'

It was just what Wise wanted to hear. He made to go but Riley caught his sleeve.

'One thing, Mickey,' he said, 'go straight there. Don't even think about having a word with those coppers on the bridge. Our foreign friend is going to take a good British hammering before we hand him over, courtesy of me and the Professor. Do you catch my drift?'

Wise nodded.

'Right,' said Riley. 'Now clear off.'

He turned to Craig.

'It's just us now, Prof. At least we mean what we say.'

Craig nodded and led the way along the path.

Anthony searched through the rest of his photographs, willing his suspicions to be wrong, then he found one of the photographs he had taken by the village hall. There it was again. Parked by St Thomas's church, just up the road from where Farid and Imogen had been sitting in the village hall, was a green Hillman Imp.

'Craig!' Anthony murmured, his throat so tight he could barely breathe. 'Dear God, it's Craig!'

He started to tremble.

'What have I done?'

Nine

Farid sat up.

'Who's there?' he said.

The chains jangled. A heavy tread could be heard on the rotting planks outside.

Farid scrambled to his feet and made for the door, but a figure blocked his way, silhouetted against the early evening sun.

'Who are you?' Farid asked.

His stomach clenched with fear.

'I've got him, Prof,' said Riley.

'What do you want?' Farid asked.

It was a stupid question. Riley had already reached for one of the chains hanging from the roof timber. A second man appeared. He too armed himself with a rusting chain.

'Please don't hurt me,' said Farid. 'I will give myself up. I won't resist you.'

'Oh, come on,' said Riley. 'Don't spoil our fun. We *want* you to resist.'

Farid frowned.

'I don't understand.'

'Do you want me to translate, Abdul?' Riley sneered.

He swung the chain at the wall of the boathouse. The whole construction shuddered.

'Understand that?'

Farid drew back.

'I've already told you I will give myself up,' Farid said. 'What more do you want?'

'Maybe we should show you,' Riley said, 'seeing as you don't understand plain English. You first, Professor.'

Without another word, Craig took a step forward and swung the chain at Farid. It smashed into his shoulder and laid him out on the ground, screaming in pain. Farid looked up. His attacker's eyes were blue, like the sky reflected through ice.

'Here!' Anthony screamed at Mum. 'Stop here!'

He was burning with an energy born of despair and something else too – atonement. He could see Farid's dark eyes staring into the core of his being. They flashed an accusation at him.

Anthony's inner voice came back with the kind of certainty he had never felt before: it's up to me to prevent this evil from going any further.

Mum stopped the car in a plume of blue-black tyre smoke. Ahead of her she could see the police on the bridge. The attention of one of them was attracted by the squeal of brakes.

'Anthony,' said Mum. 'Are you going to tell me what this is about?'

'It's The Boys, Mum. They think Farid hurt Imogen.'

Mum's eyes were slow to register understanding.

'The escaped asylum seeker, Mum. They've put the blame on him. If we don't stop them they could kill him.'

Anthony jumped out of the car and started running towards the lake.

'Anthony!' Mum called. 'Where are you going? I don't understand.'

'The Boys,' Anthony cried. 'They're going after Farid.

He's in the boathouse. Tell the police. For God's sake, hurry!'

With that, he vanished among the trees.

'My turn, Prof,' said Riley, stepping forward.

But Craig shrugged him away, surprising Riley with his strength, and swung the chain again. Only by rolling to his left did Farid escape the chain smashing into his skull.

'What are you doing, Prof?' said Riley, horrified. 'We said we were going to teach the beggar a lesson, not kill him.'

But Craig was out of control. He wrapped the chain tighter round his fist and swung it at Farid's head. It struck him a glancing blow. Pain flashed through Farid's jaw. Blood spurted from the wound.

'Not his head!' Riley screamed. 'You'll kill him.'

'Get out,' said Craig, his voice an octave lower and a whole world darker.

'What?'

Eyes black as eternity stared into Riley.

'I said get out. Go back to the Inn if you want. I'll handle this.'

'You're crazy!' said Riley. 'You're completely crazy.'

Craig didn't even turn his eyes. He didn't need anybody now.

'Oh, go home, Peter. Go and hold Mickey's hand. I'm the only one who can do this for Imogen. I won't tell the police you were here.'

Riley did as he was told. He was confused. A man who had been a complete joke was now ordering them about like schoolboys. As he walked bewildered along the side of the lake he became aware of the chain in his hand.

'Hell's teeth!' he murmured. 'I could go down for this.'

With one swing he threw it into the water.

Anthony burst from the woods, skidding on the damp leaf mould. He saw Riley walking away, shoulders hunched, and then turned his gaze towards the boathouse. Through the doorway he saw a man's back, then an arm rising to strike. Craig.

'No!' he screamed. 'Leave him alone!'

Lungs bursting, Anthony ran to the boathouse door. Craig was standing over Farid. He had him by the throat. He was snarling something into his face.

'I loved her!' he was saying. 'Me! I'm the only one who really cares.'

Anthony heard the words and his heart turned cold.

Those words, I've said them myself.

But there, he knew, the similarity ended. This man had succumbed to his hurt, allowed it to own him. Anthony had made mistakes, but it was still in his hands to put them right.

'Please,' Farid said, his voice bubbling through a mouthful of blood. 'I've done nothing wrong. Why do you want to hurt me?'

Craig slammed his head down on to the wooden floor and raised the chain. Anthony seized his chance and threw himself at Craig. They fell heavily into the far wall. Pain slashed through Anthony's jarred shoulder, but his action had done its job. Startled to be thrown off balance, Craig twisted round to see who had attacked him.

He saw a ghost boy.

Anthony was crouched over the semi-conscious Farid, shielding him from a possible renewed attack, when he heard footsteps.

'Stay away!' he cried, flailing weakly with his left arm. 'You won't hurt him. I won't let you.'

'It's all right,' said his Mum. 'It's me.'

Anthony looked up. She was framed in the doorway. Behind her stood two police officers, a man and a woman.

'Did you see him?' Anthony asked. 'Did you see Craig?'

Mum shook her head.

'He's gone.'

'It was him, Mum. He's the one who attacked Imogen.'

'Mr Craig did? You're sure about this? He's always been such a quiet man.'

'I've got photographs,' said Anthony. 'You can see for yourself. Besides, look what he's done to Farid.'

The mention of Imogen's name seemed to drag Farid up from the black waters of oblivion.

'Imogen,' he croaked hoarsely. 'What's happened to her?'

'Just rest,' Mum said, kneeling beside him.

She glanced at the police officers.

'Can you call an ambulance?'

Tim Bayliss was sitting on a low brick wall in front of the hospital when the ambulance pulled up. He sipped from a styrofoam cup and stared straight ahead. He had no interest in the comings and goings of the hospital, not when his daughter was undergoing an operation which could mean life or death. He was about to go back inside when he heard the trundle of the gurney's wheels on the tarmac. Something made him look up. The moment he saw Farid he rushed forward, throwing the cup aside.

'What did you do to my daughter?' he yelled.

A policeman stepped in front of him.

'Let me go!' Tim cried. 'Do you know what he's done?'

Then a voice broke through his anguish and his rage.

'It wasn't him, Mr Bayliss.'

He focused on Anthony's white face.

'It wasn't Farid,' Anthony said. 'It was Craig.'

'Craig?' Tim repeated. 'Who the hell is Craig?'

Then he remembered.

'The contractor?' he gasped. 'The one she said was like an uncle?'

Anthony nodded. Mrs Hewlett was with him. They had followed the ambulance in her car.

'Is there any news about Imogen?' she asked.

Tim shook his head.

'We're waiting,' he said. 'It's all we can do.'

Barry Hewlett had just taken a call from his wife when the police arrived.

'You want to see Mr Craig?' Hewlett said.

He was still trying to make sense of what she'd told him about their guest.

'Shall I take you up now?'

The officers nodded. With Trixie clattering up the stairs ahead of him, Hewlett led the way to Craig's room.

'It just goes to show,' Hewlett said, 'it's always the ones you don't expect.'

One of the officers knocked.

'Mr Craig?'

Another knock.

'OK, Mr Hewlett, open up.'

He slipped the key in the lock.

'But he's such a quiet man.'

'If you could just open the door please, sir,' said one of the CID officers.

'Of course.'

He opened the door and stepped back. That's when he saw Craig.

'Dear God!'

The Professor was hanging by his belt from one of the

beams that crossed the ceiling. Hewlett saw his face then looked away. The shadow of the body turned slowly on the floor.

There would be no need for a confession.

MARSHAM OBSERVER
Thursday, September 26

MARSHAM GIRL'S ORDEAL AT AN END

A Marsham girl who was the victim of a brutal attack came home from hospital yesterday. Sixteen-year-old Imogen Bayliss spent three weeks in a coma after the attack. She will now complete her convalescence at home.

Her mother, Mrs Karen Bayliss, said: 'Imogen has been through a terrible ordeal. She was the victim of an unprovoked attack. We are just hoping we can put all this behind us and get on with our lives.'

Imogen's attacker, 50-year-old Gordon Craig, a self-employed electrician from the West Midlands, was found hanging in his hotel bedroom shortly after the incident.

A police spokesman said: 'We are confident that nobody else was involved in this appalling attack on a young girl. The case is now closed.'

Epilogue

Tim Bayliss came upstairs about twenty past nine. It was a beautiful autumn morning. Ochre light bathed the walls of Imogen's room. At the sound of his tread Imogen looked up from the computer. She was wearing a headscarf. A few strands of her blonde hair peeked out. The scarf was something she would be keeping on until her hair grew back over the patch shaved before her operation. She fingered the material self-consciously.

'Ready for school tomorrow?' Dad asked.

'I don't know,' Imogen said. 'Maybe. I'm a bit nervous though. I've hardly set foot outside since the incident.'

Imogen always chose her words carefully. The last thing she wanted to call it was the attack.

'You'll be fine,' Dad said.

He handed her an envelope.

'You've got a letter.'

Imogen saw the Frankfurt postmark and ran her thumb over it.

'Germany,' Dad said. 'It must be Farid.'

He stood watching for a few moments then took the hint.

'I'll be going then. Do you want anything?'

'No, that's all right, Dad,' Imogen replied. 'I'm fine.'

Even after he had gone, she didn't immediately open the letter. For a long while she just held it and looked out of her window towards the village hall. Then she walked downstairs and out into the garden. She could feel her parents' eyes on her but neither of them said a word. There had been a lot of talk lately about *giving her space*. She lifted her face to the breeze and let it move over her skin. She closed her eyes and felt the cool air on her eyelids. Who knows where she was for those few moments? Then, returning to this place and this time, she glanced at the envelope and tore it open.

A minibus was turning left off the High Street into Kiddington Road. It passed Imogen in the garden. Instinctively, Anthony looked out of the window. For an instant his eyes met Imogen's but she looked away immediately. Then she was gone. It was only the second time Anthony had seen her since the attack. He had called at the Bayliss's house once to ask how she was. He had glimpsed her standing behind her mother but she hadn't wanted to talk to him. He wasn't surprised. He had hoped for forgiveness, but life isn't always like that.

He unzipped his bag and looked at his camera. He didn't take it out, however. He would be saving it for shots of Kiddington Castle. That was what he used his camera for these days. He tried to capture the remnants of days gone by, or images of timeless landscapes. After the castle it would be into the town for something to eat and a visit to the library. Then it would be a matter of killing the rest of the day until the afternoon bus came. Not too much of a problem, he thought – not for somebody who was used to his own company.

Imogen unfolded Farid's letter and read:

Dear Imogen,

They are moving us tomorrow, so by the time you read this I will be looking out at the world from a different window. What you get to see is pretty much the same though, the same suburbs, the same hostile eyes. My surroundings won't matter very much. The window will not look out on Kiddington or Marsham. I won't see you.

I hope you are fully recovered. My jaw still hurts some-times, though I know it could have been much worse. That man could have killed both of us.

I am not sure whether I ought to write to you again. I feel the same way I always did. It will break my heart never to see you again, but I know they will never let me back into Britain, so what would be the point of torturing myself with more letters? The dreams we had are gone for ever. Maybe we should face facts and accept that our lives will take different directions from now on. It tears me apart to say this, my beautiful Imogen, but I think I will never see you again. You must forget me.

Goodbye.

Your friend and love,
Farid.

Imogen read the letter twice before folding it and slipping it into the pocket of her jeans. She left her fingers touching the material a minute then turned, walked to the house and gave a final glance in the direction of the woods. She would not be able to write back to Farid. She didn't have his address.

She wasn't sure if she would write even if she did have it.

I saw Smith and Jones at the castle, Tara too. It must be one of their hangouts. I didn't shoot them though. I just took a few pictures of the castle and left. I don't shoot people any more.

Also by Alan Gibbons

THE LEGENDEER TRILOGY

The Shadow of the Minotaur

'Real life' or the death defying adventures of the Greek myths, with their heroes and monsters, daring deeds and narrow escapes – which would you choose?

For Phoenix it's easy. He hates his new home and the new school where he is bullied. He's embarrassed by his computer geek dad. But when he logs on to The Legendeer, the game his dad is working on, he can be a hero. He is Theseus fighting the terrifying Minotaur, or Perseus battling with snake-haired Medusa.

The trouble is The Legendeer is more than just a game. Play it if you dare.

Vampyr Legion

What if there are real worlds where our nightmares live and wait for us?

Phoenix has found one and it's alive. Armies of bloodsucking vampyrs and terrifying werewolves, the creatures of our darkest dreams, are poised to invade our world.

But Phoenix has encountered the creator of *Vampyr Legion*, the evil Gamesmaster, before and knows that this deadly computer game is for real – he must win or never come back.

Warriors of the Raven

The game opens up the gateway between our world and the world of the myths.

The Gamesmaster almost has our world at his mercy. Twice before fourteen-year-old Phoenix has battled against him in *Shadow of the Minotaur* and *Vampyr Legion*, but *Warriors of the Raven* is the game at its most complex and deadly level. This time, Phoenix enters the arena for the final conflict, set in the world of Norse myth. Join Phoenix in Asgard to fight Loki, the Mischief-maker, the terrifying Valkyries, dragons and fire demons – and hope for victory. Our future depends on him.

Julie and Me . . . and Michael Owen Makes Three

It's been a year of own goals for Terry.

– Man U, the entire focus of his life (what else is there?), lose to arch-enemies Liverpool FC

– he looks like Chris Evans, no pecs

– Mum and Dad split up (just another statistic)

– he falls seriously in love with drop dead gorgeous Julie. It's bad enough watching Frisky Fitzy (school golden boy) drool all over her, but worse still she's an ardent Liverpool FC supporter.

Life as Terry knows it is about to change in this hilariously funny, sometimes sad, utterly readable modern Romeo and Juliet story.

Julie and Me: Treble Trouble

For one disastrous year Terry has watched Julie, the girl of his dreams, go out with arch rival Frisky Fitz, seen his Mum and Dad's marriage crumble and his beloved Man U go the same way. 2001 has got to be better.

– Will he get to run his hands through the lovely Julie's raven tresses?

– What happens when his new streamlined Mum gets a life?

– Can Man U redeem themselves and do the business in the face of the impossible?

Returning the love – that's what it's all about.

Read the concluding part of *Julie and Me* and all will be revealed.

The Edge

Danny is a boy on the edge. A boy teetering on the brink of no return, living in fear.

Cathy is his mother. She's been broken by fear.

Chris Kane is fear – and they belong to him.

But one day they escape. They're looking for freedom, for the promised land where they can start really living. Instead they find prejudice, and danger of another kind.

Uncompromising and disturbing, but utterly readable, Alan Gibbons' novel positively crackles with tension as he writes about a mother and her son desperate to start a new life.

Caught in the Crossfire

'*You know what happens to people like you? You get hit in the crossfire.*'

Shockwaves sweep the world in the aftermath of 11 September. The Patriotic League barely need an excuse in their fight to get Britain back for the British, but this is chillingly perfect.

Rabia and Tahir are British Muslims, Daz and Jason are out looking for trouble, Mike and Liam are brothers on different sides. None of them will escape unscarred from the terrifying and tragic events which will weave their lives together.

Marking a new dimension in his writing on race, riots and real life *Caught in the Crossfire* is an unforgettable novel that Alan Gibbons needed to write.

'Gibbons' writing often addresses worrying issues of social justice but never as powerfully as in this novel . . . the writing – short, sharp pieces that take us into the mind of each character – is accessible and compulsive.' Wendy Cooling, *The Bookseller*

'Gibbons handles his large cast of characters skilfully. The story rattles along, building up suspense and complexity without ever becoming confusing . . . Gibbons . . . writes with passionate conviction . . .' Gillian Cross, *The Guardian*